Threat of Scandal

Ayr Bray

Ayr Bray's author website is http://www.ayrbray.com.

Sign up for book updates from AYR! (http://ayrbray.com/subscribe/)

Follow Ayr on Facebook (https://www.facebook.com/ayrbray)

Follow Ayr on Twitter (https://twitter.com/AyrBray)

Novels by Ayr Bray

The Illegitimate Heir (2015)
Threat of Scandal (2014)
Pemberley Mistletoe (2013)
Hunted; I survived (2014)

Novellas by Ayr Bray

Cowardly Witness: Pemberley #1 (2015)
Pompous Schemes: Pemberley #2 (2015)
Blinded Recluse: Pemberley #3 (2015)

Scent of Desire (2015)
Felicity in Marriage (2013)
Conjugal Obligation (2013)
Magnetic (2013)

Novelettes by Ayr Bray

Not Handsome Enough (2013)
Six Inches Deep In Mud (2013)
Succession of Rain (2014)

Learn more at http://www.ayrbray.com

*Book Classifications
Novel: Over 40,000 words
Novella: 17,500-40,000 words
Novelette: 7,500-17,500 words
Short Story: Under 7,500 words

Threat of Scandal

Chapter One

London 1816

A loud rapping on the thick oak door of the London townhouse startled Georgiana Darcy from her sketching moments before Colonel Richard Fitzwilliam's urgent voice was heard in the foyer.

"Grey, where is my cousin? I must speak to him immediately."

Georgiana left her easel and went to the sitting room door, anxious to know why her cousin seemed so distressed.

"Mr. Darcy is in his study, Colonel," the butler replied. "Would you like me to announce you?"

"No, I will announce myself."

Georgiana peered into the hall just in time to see her cousin hasten into the study, his dark red military cloak swirling behind him. The door closed with a boom, making her jump.

Returning to her easel with a puzzled frown, Georgiana spent above a quarter of an hour fiddling with her pencils. She was unable to concentrate; she could not help but wonder what her cousin and brother were discussing. Abandoning her easel once more, she stood at the window looking out at the picturesque garden copse at the side of the house, the very scene she had been attempting to sketch. Last night's rain had left droplets of water clinging to the branches of the budding shade trees, and songbirds were returning from their winter away. The pleasant aspect that had so captivated Georgiana this morning held no charm for her now as she pondered the possible reasons for Richard's apparent distress.

She remained thus for some time, lost in unpleasant speculation, until the sound of someone entering the sitting room drew her from her thoughts.

"Good morning, Georgiana. I trust you slept well." Elizabeth Darcy, Georgiana's sister-in-law, took a seat in her favourite chair near the fire.

"Yes, Elizabeth, I did. How are you this morning?"

"I am well, thank you. I was just reading a letter from Miss Hazel about the children. I miss them dearly."

"As do I. What news from Longbourn?"

"Miss Hazel writes that little Jane is completely weaned off pap and is now eating solids. My mother is most happy about this. It seems Grandmamma Bennet has taken to carrying biscuits in a little drawstring pouch with which she expertly bribes the children for kisses."

"I can very easily imagine Mrs. Bennet doing just that," Georgiana said.

"Miss Hazel also reports that now the weather has turned for the better Grandpapa Bennet takes little Bennet with him almost everywhere. The two of them are inseparable; Bennet is hardly in the nursery anymore."

"I am sure Bennet is most happy to be with his Grandpapa Bennet. Those two are an adorable set."

"I agree. I wonder if my father would have behaved the same way had he had a son."

"I am certain he would have."

"You will never guess what else. Miss Hazel said my mother has asked her to bring Bennet and Jane to breakfast with her and my father every morning. Can you believe it?"

"It does seem a little unusual, but then again, they are used to a full and active household and now it is just the two of them. Perhaps the commotion of two young children seems a little more normal to them."

"You must be correct. I know the marriage of all her daughters has calmed my mother's nerves, but to willingly bring toddlers to the breakfast room on a daily basis is almost too unusual to comprehend. But Miss Hazel is an honest creature, so it must be true."

Elizabeth looked at the small clock on the mantle before asking, "Have you already had your breakfast?"

"Yes, I was up quite early this morning. I think I have sufficiently recovered from our late night at the Harrisons' ball last Saturday."

"What about your brother? Have you seen him this morning?"

"He is in his study with Richard."

"Richard?" Elizabeth sat forward, evidently surprised. "Is he here?"

"Yes, he arrived about half an hour ago. He was in a great hurry and went straight in to speak with Fitzwilliam. They've been sequestered in the study ever since." A tingling sensation swept up and down Georgiana's spine. Something must be gravely amiss. She walked to the chair opposite Elizabeth, but did not sit; her mounting sense of unease would not allow her to relax.

Elizabeth's eyes darted to the door. "Well, I'm sure we will see them as soon as they have concluded their business. You know how men can be. Why don't you take a seat?"

Georgiana sat down. "Lizzy, Richard arrived in quite a state. He barely said a word to Mr. Grey and he did not even remove his cloak. In addition, he slammed the door to Fitzwilliam's study. He never slams the door."

"Never?" Elizabeth raised an eyebrow. "I can think of at least three times he has slammed doors. I think he visits in such a state at least twice a year or so, does he not?"

"I suppose you are right," Georgiana admitted.

"Do not worry, Georgie. I am certain if something is the matter your brother will inform us. For all we know, their business was done in five minutes and they are now discussing the breeding of hunting dogs."

Georgiana wished she could so easily justify the men's absence as Elizabeth, but she could not.

"Did your brother eat with you?" Elizabeth asked.

"No, he did not. He told me he was going to wait for you and went straight to his study."

Elizabeth smiled sweetly. "Yes, that is what I thought he would do. I shall wait to go in to breakfast until he is ready."

"My brother will not fault you for going in to breakfast without him. I am sure he could not have known Richard would arrive and take up his entire morning."

"I suppose you are right," Elizabeth said. "I know you said you already ate, but perhaps you would like to keep me company?"

Georgiana followed Elizabeth into the breakfast room where Elizabeth filled her plate and Georgiana poured herself a cup of tea.

*D*arcy and Richard emerged from the study three quarters of an hour later. Richard took his leave in the hall, promising to meet Darcy at the appointed time and place.

Georgiana looked towards the door in time to see him hurry past without so much as a good morning to her or Elizabeth. It was so unlike him not to at least say hello and kiss her cheek. He always had time for her.

In an instant, a memory of the only other time her cousin had arrived in such a state, sequestered himself with her brother in his study, and then left without taking his leave flashed through her mind. It had happened little more than five years ago, when she had been younger and a great deal more naïve about men in general. A chill ran up her spine at the horrible memory of the almost-elopement with George Wickham. *Thank God*, thought Georgiana, *they do not have to deal with something like that again.*

It may not be something so serious, but she knew her brother and cousin far too well to suppose it was only a trivial matter. Something was definitely wrong.

Darcy strode briskly into the breakfast room. He rushed to the sideboard, threw some food onto a plate, and took his seat. Georgiana was shocked he had loaded his plate in such a sloppy manner. As Elizabeth poured him a cup of tea, he said, "Elizabeth, I am glad you came in to breakfast. I apologize for not being here to join you."

"It is al—"

"I cannot accompany you to the bookshop like we had planned. In fact, I'm afraid you're going to have to cancel your plans for today. As will you, Georgiana." Elizabeth had looked surprised when Darcy cut her off. Something must have distressed him greatly, as he had never been so uncaring of what she would say. She no longer attempted to speak, but the worry lines creased her forehead.

Georgiana's hands lay clasped in her lap, fear nipping at the edge of her senses.

"You and Georgiana must stay here at the townhouse. You are not to go out of doors or accept any visitors until Richard or I tell you it is safe to do so."

"Safe!" Elizabeth gasped, her hand flying to her chest.

"Yes." Fitzwilliam chewed his food rapidly, his breakfast disappearing off the plate faster than it ever had before.

Observing her brother's unusual behaviour, Georgiana became scared. He never acted so improperly. He never interrupted what she or Elizabeth was saying. He never rushed his meals. He never ordered them about. She was afraid of what he would say next.

Georgiana and Elizabeth watched in silence while Fitzwilliam finished his meal and then stood. "Elizabeth, please walk with me upstairs."

Elizabeth followed Fitzwilliam from the room. Georgiana remained seated, a cold, hard knot forming in the pit of her stomach.

Georgiana paced back and forth across the intricately woven rug in the centre of the sitting room while she waited for Elizabeth and Fitzwilliam to return.

The house was silent, as if everyone knew something was amiss. She had yet to see the housekeeper, Mrs. Grey, or any of the servants outside of the breakfast room. Normally she liked the quiet and solitude of days like this, but today it brought an eerie feeling and she shivered despite the fires being stoked against the February chill.

Hearing commotion on the stairs, Georgiana stopped pacing and watched the door expectantly.

When Elizabeth and Fitzwilliam rushed past but did not enter the sitting room, Georgiana followed them to the foyer.

Mr. Grey was helping Fitzwilliam on with his coat, hat, and gloves while he issued instructions to Elizabeth.

"Remember what I said. No visitors. I do not care who they are or how well you know them. No one is to enter this house except Richard or myself."

"I understand." Elizabeth stretched up on tiptoes, kissed her husband, and whispered something to him before stepping back and allowing him to race out the door to his waiting horse.

"Elizabeth, what is going on?" Georgiana asked after the door closed behind him. "Why is my brother acting so strangely?"

Elizabeth looped her arm through Georgiana's and guided her into the sitting room. When they had settled on the settee, Elizabeth spoke. "I cannot be sure of the details, but I understand Richard overheard some information about a member of our family that requires immediate attention. Have no fear; your brother will take care of everything. He always does."

"I hope everyone is all right," Georgiana said. "It is so unpleasant to be sick, and it would distress me greatly if someone was injured. But why would Fitzwilliam ask us to stay in and not accept visitors if that is the case?"

Elizabeth picked up her embroidery without responding.

"Elizabeth?" Georgiana questioned warily.

Elizabeth made a couple of tight stitches on her sampler before looking up with an unconvincing smile.

"Elizabeth, you know more. I am sure of it." Elizabeth did not reply, but rather she returned to her embroidery with an interest she rarely displayed. "I am not a child anymore," Georgiana exclaimed. "I am twenty years old. I do not see why Fitzwilliam thinks he cannot tell me his troubles. If something is the matter with someone in our family I should be informed."

When Elizabeth remained silent, Georgiana stamped her foot and stalked to the window.

"If you are not careful, I will accuse you of taking too many lessons from Lydia," Elizabeth scolded her normally prim and proper sister.

Georgian sighed. "I suppose you are right. I do not know what has come over me. It is just …" Georgiana's voice trailed off.

"Why don't we go into the music room so you can play for me? A little music is all you need to calm your nerves." Elizabeth tucked her sampler into her sewing basket. "It will be a long day if all we do is fret over something neither of us has any control over or knowledge of."

"I suppose you are right," Georgiana said, following Elizabeth into the adjacent music room.

Elizabeth took her seat by the little window that overlooked the gardens while Georgiana took hers at the piano and practiced her favourite pieces by Mozart.

The simple act of playing song after song had a calming effect on Georgiana, and soon her anxiety over the morning's events faded.

"Elizabeth, I think you had the right idea when you asked me to play. I feel much better," Georgiana announced half an hour later.

"Wonderful," Elizabeth said. "Now, why don't we have some tea and write our letters? I have yet to respond to Jane's letter from last Wednesday. I'm sure she will think I am ill and rush to town if she does not hear from me very soon."

Elizabeth and Georgiana took their tea together in the sitting room and then parted ways, Elizabeth intent on her letter writing and Georgiana retiring to the library to read.

She didn't go directly to the shelves to select a book, but rather went to the window to take in the street view. She had often found interesting subjects to sketch on the busy side street below. The heavy drapes were drawn, and she parted the light lace coverings to expose the glass beyond. The usual carriages and men on horseback passed by their townhouse. The street was busier today than normal, and she noticed how more than one person seemed to stare at the townhouse as they went by.

Chapter Two

Georgiana and Elizabeth ate supper together in the little dining room. It was very late and still Fitzwilliam had neither returned nor sent word of his activities. The agony of not knowing was again taking its toll on Georgiana. A headache began with a slight pounding in her forehead and settled behind her eyes in continual bursts of stabbing pain.

Another storm had rolled in an hour ago. The wind howled and the rain rapped against the dining room windows. A loud noise at the front of the house made Georgiana jump in her seat. The commotion increased, and she and Elizabeth, in silent accord, raced to the hallway to investigate. The sound of her brother's heavy footsteps in the foyer made Georgiana's pulse race. *Soon we will know something*, she thought.

"Fitzwilliam," Elizabeth exclaimed, rushing to his side. "You are soaked through." Turning to the footman, she said, "Take Mr. Darcy's coat and tell Mrs. Grey to send up a supper tray and tea directly."

The footman dashed to do as he was bid.

Fitzwilliam paused on his way up the stairs and turned to look at his sister. "Georgie, give me one hour and then meet me in my study. I have something I must speak to you about."

"Your study?" Georgiana was surprised. Her brother rarely asked her into his study. They generally conversed in the library where it was more comfortable. Something truly grim must have occurred for Fitzwilliam to summon her to his study. "Of course, brother."

The door to her brother's study was open when she approached at the appointed time, and she could see him and Elizabeth sitting together in the room. Fitzwilliam stood to greet her as she entered and closed the door behind her. Then, taking her by the hand, he led her to the couch next to Elizabeth and helped her sit. Rather than taking a seat behind his desk as Georgiana expected him to, he took a seat on her other side. He did not speak right away, but rubbed his palms on his knees.

"Fitzwilliam," Georgiana began hesitantly, "are you all right?" Georgiana's heart raced as she looked at her brother's face and saw despair in his eyes.

He shook his head and cleared his throat. Georgiana swallowed, waiting for the worst. By now she was fully expecting news that someone in her family had died. "Georgie dear," he began, taking one of her delicate hands in his own, "I'm afraid I have some bad news."

"Bad news," Georgiana murmured, forcing her

mind to pay heed to every word he spoke.

"Yes, dearest, news of the gravest nature." Darcy's voice broke as he continued. "First, I must ask: are you acquainted with the Duke of Rothford?"

"No, I have never heard of him." She was confused by his question, wondering how a peer outside their sphere could possibly be connected to her family. "Do you know him, brother?"

"Not personally, no, but I am aware of who he is."

"What does he have to do with your news?" Georgiana asked.

"Yesterday morning, Richard was at breakfast with some officers and heard a rumour that you were found in a compromising position with the Duke of Rothford in the library at the Harrisons' ball on Saturday night."

All colour drained from Georgiana's complexion. "You cannot be serious." She looked between her brother and Elizabeth, searching for any hint that she had misunderstood his words.

"Unfortunately, I am very serious."

"Brother, I have never been in the Harrisons' library. I stayed in the public rooms." Georgiana brought her hand to her forehead, trying to remember all that had taken place at Saturday's ball. "Fitzwilliam, you know I am innocent. Elizabeth, you were with me all night. Surely, you know."

"Of course you are, dearest, but that is irrelevant at this time. We must discover how these rumours were started and by whom. Can you think of anything that happened that may have caused their circulation?

Anything at all?" Fitzwilliam asked.

"No. Nothing." Georgiana massaged her temples. "Wait. Elizabeth, remember when I went to refresh myself and you waited for me at the head of the hall? I told you a man had opened a door into me as I went down the hallway. After apologising, he held my left hand and raised it to inspect my upper arm and shoulder where I had been hit by the door. Upon declaring me uninjured, he bowed over my hand and I went on my way. He was standing very close to me at the time. Do you think someone could have seen and misinterpreted the action?"

"Perhaps. You say he took your hand?" Elizabeth's expression was grim.

"Just to inspect my arm, but yes, he touched me."

Elizabeth turned to Fitzwilliam. "Where is the library at the Harrisons'?"

"It is the second door on the left down the hall off the main entrance."

"Georgie, was that the room?"

"The very one."

"Well, it seems someone saw your interaction with the Duke and misinterpreted it. A rumour was begun and has spread rapidly through the Ton and beyond."

"What are we to do? Can we not explain the truth of the situation and be done with it? Surely no one believes what is being said."

"Unfortunately, they do. The Ton loves a good scandal. People in general are all too apt to believe anything, especially when it involves a wealthy lady and an eligible duke," Fitzwilliam explained.

"I am ruined." A hand as cold as death clenched her heart and squeezed the breath from her lungs. Georgiana's world was caving in around her as thoughts of the ostracism and scorn she would soon receive from everyone in London and beyond began to assail her. Already she could foresee the ramifications. She imagined her Almack's vouchers being revoked, dinner invitations cancelled, ball invitations withheld, and women crossing the street just so they would not be forced to walk past her. She gasped for air as tears began to spill from her eyes. "Brother, what is to be done? Can you and Richard remedy this?"

"We are unsure as of yet. Richard spent all of yesterday trying to locate the source of the rumours, but was unable to. Today, he and I met with the Harrisons, who assured us they have no notion of who started the rumours. We did confirm that the Duke of Rothford was on the guest list and in attendance. The Harrisons said he spent most of the evening at cards or reading in the library. Apparently, he deigned to dance only the first and last sets of the evening with the Harrisons' daughter and the daughter of a marquess whose estate neighbours his own."

"What of the Duke? Did you speak with him? Surely he can refute the rumours."

"We went to his townhouse, but he left town early Sunday. He is not expected to return until Friday. We will go to him when he returns."

"Friday! But that is a full four days away. Something must be done before then." Georgiana dabbed at her tears with her already sodden handkerchief. "What else? What else did you and Richard do?"

"We went to White's to learn the extent of the damage. It seems the news is quite widespread and no one knows the source. As of now, we are unable to quell it, but you know we will never give up."

Georgiana could think of nothing else to ask her brother while she sat silent in her chair. Her face was pale and tears flowed freely. She didn't even bother to wipe them away now.

Elizabeth took her hands. "Georgie, it is going to be all right. We will weather this storm together."

Georgiana wanted to believe Elizabeth was right, but so many women had been ruined for far less. Why, she knew of one woman who was shunned for simply falling from her horse and exposing a length of stocking. Never again was she invited to any society events. Her father even took away a portion of her dowry and gave it to her younger sister, hoping the offering would allow the girl a better chance to marry well in the wake of her elder sister's alleged indiscretions.

A sob broke free and Georgiana collapsed into her brother's arms.

Darcy held his sister and allowed her to cry. He longed to tell her something that would bring her relief, but he had no such words. The situation was grave.

Georgiana cried for a full five minutes before she could give voice to the questions racing through her mind. "Brother, what do you know about the man my name is linked with in this … scandal?" She could barely say the word.

"His Grace is the seventh Duke of Rothford near Abingdon. I went to school with his elder brother. He died many years ago in a carriage accident. The present duke inherited when his father died recently."

"What else do you know about him?" Before her brother could answer, she questioned him some more. "Does he know his name is linked with mine in this?" She refused to say the word "scandal" again. "Is he a good man? Dear God, he's not a ... rake, is he?"

The smallest smile tugged at the corners of Fitzwilliam's mouth. "No, he is not a rake, at least, not to my knowledge. If he was, I certainly would have heard it today."

"I am glad. I couldn't bear to have my name bandied about in association with a rake. Tell me more. How old is he? Brother, you must tell me something," Georgiana begged.

"Georgiana, dearest, I've told you everything. I really don't know more."

"Brother, I cannot accept that you and Richard have done everything possible. Elizabeth's sister was missing for days before she was recovered and made to marry Mr. Wickham, and it all came out better than anyone could have expected in the end. This is nothing compared to her indiscretions. I know you must be able to manage it." Desperation was evident on every feature of Georgiana's face. "You must."

Fitzwilliam shook his head. "Dearest, this is an entirely different situation. Only the family and a few friends knew of Lydia's indiscretions and they were all good enough to hush it up. This situation is the opposite. Someone is deliberately spreading these rumours. You know even if the gossip is proved untrue it is impossible to completely erase the memory of it. The damage has spread too far, too fast. Richard and I will do what we can, but tonight I can give you no more assurances beyond what I have already said. These things take time. Let us see what tomorrow brings." Fitzwilliam paused while Georgiana gave way to another fit of crying. When she had regained some measure of control, he continued. "I sent an express letter north to Abingdon with a message for the Duke."

"You wrote to him? Without introduction?"

"Yes I did, but I claimed an acquaintance with his brother. I hope he is a good man and will overlook my impropriety just this once. I had to risk it. The man was instructed to await a response. I hope we shall hear from him soon, perhaps as early as tomorrow or Wednesday."

"Very well. If we must wait, we must. May I be excused?" Georgiana longed to flee the suffocating confines of her brother's study.

"Of course." Fitzwilliam walked Georgiana to the door. "Georgie," he said, his voice quiet and comforting, "I am sorry I do not have better news and that I was unable to quell the rumours immediately. I tried everything I could think of, but they had circulated too far before we learned of them. As I said, Richard and I will not rest until this situation is resolved to everyone's satisfaction."

"I understand. Thank you for trying."

Georgiana bade him goodnight and ascended the stairs to her room. Lying on the bed, still clothed in her evening gown, she pulled a blanket over her and cried until she fell into a restless sleep.

Chapter Three

Georgiana woke with spirits as gloomy as the grey skies outside her bedroom window. Yesterday all she could think about was the impact the news would have on her position in society. Today her thoughts ran a different course. She realized it was unlikely she would ever marry, and if she did it would most certainly not be for love. What man would willingly attach himself to a woman who was part of such a dreadful scandal, even if it was untrue?

After years of observing her brother and Elizabeth, she had become determined to find a love like theirs, but now her dreams were shattering around her. Georgiana sat up in bed and rubbed her weary eyes. Salty tears soon wet her palms. Lying back against her pillows, she draped her arm over her face, shielding her eyes from the world beyond her room, beyond her home. She didn't want to face anyone, not even her brother and Elizabeth.

Gathering as much courage and strength as she

could muster, Georgiana left her bed and dressed for breakfast in her most comfortable morning gown. She descended the stairs slowly, her steps heavy with the weight of sorrow born upon her slender shoulders.

"Darcy, our only option is to buy her a husband." Georgiana's heart skipped a beat as the footman opened the breakfast room door just in time for her to hear her cousin's declaration. Halting in the doorway, she clasped her hand over her mouth to keep from crying out. Fresh tears stung her eyes.

"Begging your pardon, but I disagree," Elizabeth snapped. It was evidently a heated discussion going on at the breakfast table. "I think there are plenty of options. You are being selfish if you do not consider them all. In my opinion, it would be best if we remove Georgiana from London immediately and wait for the Ton to move on to maligning the next poor, unsuspecting soul. In a few months, six at the most, hardly anyone will remember any of this. If they do, we shall spend the following seasons in Bath, or even Brighton, rather than return to London."

With indignation rarely seen in her, Georgiana straightened her spine and entered the room to speak for herself. "I agree with Elizabeth. I will return to Pemberley. I will not allow you to buy me a husband. I would rather be a spinster destined to care for my brother's children than marry a fortune hunter."

Everyone's heads snapped around at the sound of Georgiana's determined but shaky voice. Fitzwilliam and Richard quickly stood to welcome her into the room as they exchanged hasty looks with each other.

"Good morning, Georgiana." Fitzwilliam eyed his sister warily.

"Good morning, brother," Georgiana said, though she did not think it was a good morning at all. Elizabeth handed her a plate and she began to dish up her breakfast.

Fitzwilliam turned his full attention to his sister. "We were just discussing our options for dealing with your … situation."

"It sounds as if Richard has made up his mind to marry me off to the first man destitute enough to have me for my dowry. Is that not correct, Richard?"

Richard wisely held his tongue.

Fitzwilliam was struck with a feeling of wonder over Georgiana's uncharacteristic outburst. He took it as a symptom of the terrible strain she was under and thought it best to try to placate her. "We have not made any decisions. If it came to that, however, you know Richard and I would find an honourable man to marry you. We would never hand you over to a fortune hunter. Do not you wish to marry and establish your own home and family?"

"Do not use my hopes and dreams against me," Georgiana cried. She did want those things, desperately, but was it worth giving up the freedom to choose her own husband in order to have them? What kind of life and family would she have if she had to buy a husband? If she married a man she did not love? Would the love of her children be enough to sustain her for the rest of her life?

"Brother, Richard," Georgiana said as she took a

moment to assess each, "you may think it is prudent to buy me a husband, but you know it is my greatest wish to marry for love. I refuse"—her voice was thick with unshed tears—"to give up my dreams. I have done nothing wrong. I deserve happiness." Her tears could no longer be contained. Burying her face in her hands, she tried to hide them.

"Sweetling," Richard said gently, calling Georgiana by the pet name he had given her when she was no more than five years old, "you know I admire your fortitude. Before yesterday I was willing to allow you to remain single until the man of your dreams rode in on his white horse to sweep you off your feet, but circumstances have changed."

"I do not see how they have changed. Unless the rumours are far worse than Fitzwilliam led me to believe, my virtue is still intact. If that is not the case, then I shall never be able to show my face out of doors for the mortification it would bring me."

"He did not mislead you; your reputation with regards to that is safe."

"Well, then, I do not see why I need a husband."

Elizabeth was proud of Georgiana for the courage she was displaying as she stood up to her brother and cousin. She imagined the girl could not have shown the same courage four years ago when they had first met.

"Marrying is the quickest way to quell the rumours," Richard insisted.

"And the easiest, is it not? Is that why you want to marry me off, so you don't have to deal with this any longer than you must?"

Richard was aghast. "Georgiana, you know that is not true. I do not want this rumour to ruin you, and I truly believe the quickest way to save your reputation is for you to marry."

"I disagree. I think a quick marriage would only give credit to the rumour, perhaps even confirm it in the eyes of many."

Pushing away his empty plate, Richard stood. Georgiana could see the despair in his eyes. "I have told you what I think. I will not force you to marry, but I would also not have you lose your chance at the happiness of a family and children."

"I am not of your opinion. Women in far worse positions have been able to marry and have a family. I shall just have to hope for the best."

"I am sorry I have upset you. It was not my intention." Richard nodded to Fitzwilliam and Elizabeth and took his leave without another word.

Georgiana picked at her food while Fitzwilliam and Elizabeth carried on a hushed conversation, about what Georgiana knew not, lost as she was in her own gloomy thoughts. Her heart told her she would be content to stay with her brother and Elizabeth forever. She could help with the education of her niece and nephew and any future children they may have. At the same time, her heart ripped in two when she thought of never having a child of her own, never having a little one call her mama.

Georgiana pushed her plate away, laid her head on her arms, and wept.

Elizabeth came around the table and took the seat next to her, rubbing her back while she spoke comforting words Georgiana could barely make out. The circular motions were soothing, and Georgiana submitted gratefully to her sister-in-law's ministrations.

At last, she took a deep breath and sat up. Her eyes were red and swollen, but determination shone in them. "Fitzwilliam, please make Richard see that he is wrong. I do want a family, but I have always hoped for a love match. I refuse to believe these rumours have ruined all my future chances of it. Do you understand my wishes? Will you support them?"

"Of course, my dear. We shall not discuss it again." He helped her to stand and pulled her into his brotherly embrace. "Georgiana, we shall get through this. I promise," he whispered in her ear.

Just then, there was a knock at the breakfast room door and Mr. Grey entered. "Sir, I know the family is not receiving callers; however a gentleman has arrived who is quite adamant about seeing you immediately."

"Who is it, Grey?" Fitzwilliam stepped back from Georgiana, allowing her to resume her seat.

The butler's glance at Georgiana was fleeting, but everyone noticed it. "His Grace the Duke of Rothford." Grey held out the Duke's card on a monogrammed pewter tray. "I have shown him to your study. I hope that is acceptable."

A gasp escaped from Georgiana at Mr. Grey's pronouncement. Her mind raced. *Why is he here? What does he want? Does he think this was my doing?*

Is he angry? She stared fixedly at her plate, waiting to hear her brother's response.

"I shall go to him directly," Fitzwilliam said, already on his way to his study.

After her brother left the room, Georgiana sat in silence while the breakfast dishes were cleared away. Elizabeth tried to speak with her, but found all conversation impossible.

It was a full agonising thirty minutes later when Georgiana heard her brother and the Duke in the hall. It seemed like an eternity before the door opened and her brother returned. His face was stoic as he sat and called for a fresh cup of tea. Then he dismissed the servants and instructed they close the door behind them.

"Georgiana, dearest, as you know, that was the Duke of Rothford. He has heard of the scandal, and he also received my letter. He returned to London early to speak with me. First of all, you should know how concerned he is for you. He repeatedly remarked how he could not imagine what a woman in your position must be feeling. He confirmed he was the man who collided with you in the hall at the Harrisons' ball and agrees with me that this interaction must be what started the rumours."

Georgiana's hands shook. She tried to take a sip of her tea, but her trembling made it impossible. Fitzwilliam pulled his chair to her side of the table and took her cold hands in his to steady her.

"Dearest, are you all right?"

"What else did he have to say?"

"It is his intention to refute the rumours and spread word of your innocence. He is confident that with his help this can all be cleared up in a few days."

"Do you agree? Will his denial clear my name and let us go on like this never happened?"

"Yes, I think he is right. A few well-placed words and this will all be over." Fitzwilliam's face did not hold the same assurance he tried to convey with his assertions.

"I do not believe you, brother. I do not think his word will erase the damage done to my reputation."

"Regardless, it is the best hope we have at the moment. Let us see what happens and then we will decide if additional actions are required. I have faith all will turn out well in the end."

Chapter Four

For a week, Georgiana and Elizabeth kept to the house. All callers were turned away, even Mrs. Gardiner, Elizabeth's dearest aunt, though she received an immediate letter of apology sent by way of a footman to her house in Cheapside.

Fitzwilliam met with the Duke each time a new rumour arose. By the end of the week, they had fought three separate rumours, each more vicious than the first. The second rumour accused the couple of meeting clandestinely at the Darcys' townhouse without a chaperone. When the third rumour surfaced, Fitzwilliam hated to tell his sister the details. Knowing the Ton thought she had lost her virtue to the Duke during one of their alleged private meetings was sure to spiral her into depths of depression they had not yet seen. Fitzwilliam could hardly think of the rumours without wanting to do violence upon the perpetrators.

For the life of them, they could not discover from whence these scandalous lies were originating. His

Grace owned he did have his suspicions, but he did not like to voice them without proof, and he assured Fitzwilliam there was no proof to be had despite his utmost efforts to uncover it.

Georgiana withdrew more and more as the days went by. Her mood had progressed from sad, to morose, to depressed and haunted. She lacked energy; she was not eating or sleeping well. She was frequently to be found in the library sitting in front of the fire and staring at nothing beyond the flickering blaze. Towards the end of the week she rarely took meals with the family or even changed out of her morning dress. She hardly spoke and she neglected her books, her drawing, and her music. Nothing could pull her out of her melancholy.

"Fitzwilliam, has His Grace inquired about an introduction to me?" Georgiana asked on the ninth day after she had learned of the initial rumour.

"Yes, when I first met him. Why do you ask?"

"Why have I not met him, then?"

"We determined it would be best if he remained at a distance while the rumours continued. We had hoped thus to thwart any future ones."

"I see. It seems to have made little difference. I would like to meet the Duke. It is time I left London, and I would like to thank him for all he has done before I go."

"Very well. I am meeting him again today. I will inquire whether he still wishes to form an acquaintance. If he agrees, we shall return to the house around three o'clock."

"Thank you, brother. Also, if it is agreeable to you and Elizabeth, I would like to return to Pemberley on Tuesday next. I hope if I leave here I will no longer be a target for whoever is spreading these horrible lies. I do not plan to return to London for a very long time."

Fitzwilliam agreed with her decision to leave though he deeply regretted the necessity. When the first rumour had been quelled he had rejoiced, thinking it was all over. How could he have been so wrong? He would give anything to go back in time nine days to when the first rumour was all they had to worry about. How simple it had been.

At one o'clock, Georgiana went to her rooms and asked Mary to help her dress. She could not be presented to the Duke in a plain morning gown. By three o'clock she was dressed in her most elegant visiting gown and waiting in the sitting room when her brother returned with the Duke.

The Duke of Rothford was full of confidence when he strode into the room and made a proper bow to Georgiana and Elizabeth. He looked exceedingly handsome in his tan breeches, polished Hessian boots, and overcoat. He struck an imposing figure with his muscular frame and the ladies could not help but be impressed by him. Georgiana wondered how he had earned his glorious physique. He seemed completely at ease in his unfamiliar surroundings. It was not until she looked into his warm brown eyes that she recognized in him some of the same emotions she had experienced the past several days. She could not mistake the strain she saw there.

"Your Grace, may I have the pleasure of introducing you to my wife, Mrs. Darcy, and my sister, Miss Darcy."

The ladies stood and curtsied. His answering bow was everything proper. "Ladies, it is a pleasure to meet you."

"The pleasure is ours," Elizabeth said. "Would you like to sit down?"

"Yes, thank you." The Duke moved to sit in the chair nearest Georgiana. He flipped back the tails of his coat before getting comfortable.

"Would you like a cup of tea?" Elizabeth offered, moving towards the tea service.

"Yes, please. Just milk."

"Here, Mrs. Darcy, let me." With a small smile, Georgiana prepared the Duke's tea. She hoped it would offer her the opportunity to compose her thoughts, which it did, until she realised he was watching her. With trembling hands, she handed him his cup and then poured another for her brother and Elizabeth. Finally, she prepared her own, silently thanking Providence that she had not spilled tea on the Duke's exquisite habiliments.

"Your Grace," Fitzwilliam began, "Miss Darcy would like permission to speak with you regarding recent events. Would you permit her to address you directly?"

"Of course." The Duke waved off the plate of tea cakes proffered by the footman and turned his full attention to Georgiana.

Georgiana had had no notion her brother would

turn the conversation to her so quickly. Now that the moment had come she felt quite unprepared. The Duke's intent gaze made her nervous. Taking a deep breath, she plucked up her courage.

"Thank you, Your Grace, for taking time out of your busy schedule to visit with us today."

"It is my pleasure, Miss Darcy. Mr. Darcy and I have discussed on more than one occasion whether an introduction would be prudent or not. I was unsure if my presence would cause further harm or distress you."

"Your presence will never distress me, Your Grace. The only things that distress me are the vicious lies the Ton seems set on spreading. I wished to make your acquaintance in order to thank you for your unexampled kindness to me. I have been most eager to express my gratitude for what you have done for me. I can't imagine how much pain and distress these past days must have caused you."

"I am sorry, exceedingly sorry," replied the Duke in a tone laden with emotion, "that you have ever been made to endure these heinous lies. If only I could have spared you from them."

"Thank you, Your Grace. As I said, your kindness has not gone unnoticed by me or my family, and I thank you for allowing me the chance to tell you as much."

"Mr. Darcy told me you will be leaving London soon."

"Yes, I have asked that I be allowed to return to my brother's house at Pemberley."

"When shall you leave?" the Duke asked.

Georgiana cast her eyes towards her brother, who said, "We shall leave on Tuesday, six days hence."

"Miss Darcy, would you allow me to call upon you again before your family departs to the north?"

"Of course, Your Grace." Georgiana could hardly believe what she was hearing. His Grace the Duke of Rothford was asking permission to call on her again! It was the last thing she expected.

"I am sorry you will be deprived of the remainder of the season. If I could be sure nothing untoward would happen, I would invite you to Almack's tomorrow night so you may have one last evening of pleasure before you depart."

Georgiana could not look at him and relied on Elizabeth to answer.

"That is very kind of you, Your Grace. However, we would not be able to accept your invitation even were you to offer it. The patronesses of Almack's have just yesterday informed us that they have revoked our annual vouchers."

"I see the feminine oligarchy has decided to exercise their uncontested powers. Well, I shall see about that." His face was dark and foreboding as he said, "Lady Sefton, you see, is my aunt. I believe I may safely promise you your vouchers will be reissued no later than tomorrow morning." The Duke shifted in his seat. "Sometimes I wonder at the power the Ton has given these women. Why, they dictate the very fashions we may wear. If I thought there was any chance of success, I would arrive in pantaloons rather than knee-breeches, without my ticket, at five minutes past midnight, and demand entrance, but even I would be turned away if I did such a thing."

Fitzwilliam nodded his agreement. "It seems strange to me how society's many factions can all agree to allow the patronesses of Almack's such uncontested powers. They could even venture to turn away the Duke of Wellington for a breach of rules, yet the ladies may do as they wish and come out unscathed. Nothing can be said or done to hurt their reputations or positions in society."

"Good God, why didn't I think of it before?" The Duke exclaimed. "Ladies, if you will, excuse my ungentlemanly outburst."

"Think nothing of it," Elizabeth said.

"I have just now considered that my aunt may be of some further use to me than securing merely your vouchers. Will you allow me to cut this visit short? I would ask that I be allowed to call again later this afternoon."

"Of course, Your Grace."

The duke stood and, offering the customary farewells, hastily strode out the front door and away from the townhouse.

It was a half-past six when the Duke of Rothford was shown into the drawing room by Mr. Grey.

"Your Grace, you are very welcome," Fitzwilliam said, standing and bowing to the Duke.

The ladies curtsied, and after everyone was seated

the Duke turned to Elizabeth.

"I have a letter for you, Mrs. Darcy. It is from my aunt, Lady Sefton." He pulled an envelope with a heavy wax seal from his inner coat pocket and handed it to Elizabeth.

"Thank you, Your Grace." Elizabeth began to set the letter aside, but he forestalled her.

"There is no need to wait for privacy; you may read it now," he instructed.

Everyone was silent as Elizabeth broke the seal and read the contents.

"Lady Sefton has reinstated our vouchers and requested we attend Almack's tomorrow night with His Grace. She further requests that Miss Darcy be presented to her. Thank you, Your Grace. We are most grateful for your interference in this matter."

"Are you well, Miss Darcy?" The Duke asked, having noticed how Georgiana's complexion had paled as Elizabeth spoke.

"Thank you, I am well. I am a little shocked at Lady Sefton's request, that is all."

"Yes, well, it was as I suspected; a little diplomacy was all that was required. I explained the entirety of your situation to my aunt and, though many women have been turned away for less, she has agreed to grant me a single favour. I shall present Miss Darcy to my aunt, who will accept her company for fifteen minutes, after which the two of us shall dance. I suspect this shall be all that is required to right all of the past week's wrongs, do you not agree?"

"Indeed I do," replied Elizabeth. "Everyone

knows the patronesses of Almack's would never allow a lady of questionable character admittance. Miss Darcy being presented to any one of their notice will undeniably prove her innocence to everyone."

"You have expressed my sentiments exactly." The Duke looked at Georgiana, who was still recovering from the shock of his aunt's request. "Miss Darcy, I hope you do not object to my interference. When the idea came to me, I knew I must attempt it."

"I do not object. Thank you for your thoughtfulness. I hope your plan will be successful."

"I am sure it will. Now, I must depart so that I can make arrangements for tomorrow evening. I shall call at ten-thirty to collect you. By the time we arrive at Almack's a sufficient crowd should be in attendance to bear witness to our little display. Until tomorrow, then." With that, the Duke made his departure for the second time that day.

Chapter Five

Georgiana stood in front of the mirror and practised a few smiles while she waited for Mary to come help her dress for her presentation to Lady Sefton. Each smile looked more forced than the one before. With a sigh, she gave up as Mary entered with the freshly pressed gown. The maid helped her dress and deftly styled her hair in the latest French fashion. Normally the pair talked while Mary worked, but tonight her mistress was too preoccupied. Mary could well understand why. There wasn't a soul below stairs who hadn't heard of the terrible rumours, though none gave any credit to them, Mary especially. She longed to say so to her beloved young mistress, but she respected her unspoken wishes and worked in silence.

Mary was just finishing Georgiana's hair when there was a knock upon the door. Mary opened it to let in Elizabeth, who carried a midnight blue velvet jewellery box to Georgiana's dressing table.

"You look wonderful," Elizabeth said, admiring how the shimmering amethyst silk of Georgiana's gown made her skin look flawless. "Your beauty could hardly be enhanced, but I think you should wear these all the same." Elizabeth opened the velvet box, revealing a set of diamonds that had belonged to Georgiana's mother.

She opened the clasp of the necklace and wrapped it around Georgiana's slender neck. The stones felt cool against her skin. Elizabeth then fastened the bracelet over Georgiana's glove. Next came the diamond hairpins, which Mary artfully arranged in her coiffure.

Georgiana glanced at herself in the mirror, touching the tips of the exquisite diamonds. Never had she been allowed to wear the Darcy diamonds. Many of the family jewels had been passed to her upon her mother's death, but the diamonds had been kept aside as a wedding present to the future Mrs. Darcy. Though Georgiana had always admired them, she had never asked Elizabeth for permission to wear them. They were far too precious.

"You are the best sister," Georgiana said as she wrapped her arms around Elizabeth and clung to her.

"Nonsense! I'm surprised you can even put up with me. I'm sure no one ever dragged you around London as I have the past few years."

"I love it. I wouldn't have it any other way."

"Come, let us go downstairs. Your anxious brother is waiting for us."

Georgiana looked in the mirror a final time and

noticed how pale her skin was against the rich colour of her gown. The strain of the past few days was more evident than she wished it to be. She tried to bring out some colour by pinching her cheeks, but it hardly helped. With another sigh, she steeled her emotions and hid behind a mask of tranquillity she was determined to maintain all evening.

Descending the stairs with Elizabeth, she heard Mr. Grey announce, "The Duke of Rothford's carriage has arrived."

"Is my sister ready?" Fitzwilliam asked.

"I am," Georgiana responded as she and Elizabeth glided into the room.

"You look beautiful, my dear," Fitzwilliam said to his wife. Then, turning to Georgiana, he said, "Georgie, I almost didn't recognize you. You look more radiant than ever."

"Thank you, brother. Shall we go?" Georgiana said as she put on her cloak.

She had just finished tying her bonnet under her chin when the Duke rapped on the door with his cane. As Mr. Grey opened it, she heard his deep, rich voice. Butterflies swirled in her stomach when the door swung wider to allow his entrance. He looked every inch a duke in his black evening coat, knee-breeches, and starched cravat. Her eyes met his, and all her worries temporarily melted away as her heart thumped so loudly in her chest she feared everyone could hear it.

"Good evening," the Duke said, and bowed.

Georgiana lowered her eyes and curtsied as she

returned his greeting.

"Shall we be off?"

"Yes, of course," Georgiana said, taking her shawl from Mary and then accepting the Duke's offered arm. Stepping into the cool night air, she inhaled the rich scent of his soap that wafted to her on the breeze.

"You look exceedingly well this evening," the Duke said, a glint of appreciation in his eye as he handed her into the carriage.

"Thank you, Your Grace," Georgiana murmured, still unable to look him in the eye for any length of time.

Elizabeth took her seat next to Georgiana and the gentlemen sat across from them. Once they were settled, the Duke tapped on the roof with his cane and the carriage smoothly took off.

Georgiana was not required to say much on the drive to Almack's, as the Duke and her brother were engaged nearly the whole journey in speculation about the evening's upcoming events. Their constant but vague references to the rumours about her and the Duke brought the colour to her cheeks that she had so desperately tried to pinch into them earlier.

Their progression was slow, as it seemed all of London was attending the ball tonight. They joined a long line of carriages conveying gaily dressed ladies and gentlemen to the doors of Almack's. The closer they got, the more nervous Georgiana became. When at last it was their turn to disembark, so deep in thought was she that she failed to notice the carriage door was open.

"Miss Darcy." She could hear the insistent voice of her brother, but she could hardly swim through the haze of her clouded mind to attend to him. "Georgiana, His Grace is offering you his hand to help you from the carriage."

Forcing her attention to the present, Georgiana blinked a few times and then accepted the Duke's outstretched hand.

"Take a deep breath. All will be well," she heard Elizabeth whisper. The Duke of Rothford gently helped her step down to the kerb. The carriage swayed under her movement and she hoped it masked her shaking, but she doubted it.

When their cloaks had been left at the entrance, they took their place in line and waited to be announced. Georgiana could feel the constant stares and whispers behind fans as their party made it to the front of the line. "His Grace the Duke of Rothford and Miss Georgiana Darcy." They walked into the room, the Duke's strong arm offering her the support she so desperately needed. "Mr. and Mrs. Fitzwilliam Darcy."

Silence wafted through the room and all eyes turned to them. This was the moment Georgiana dreaded, the moment when she was the centre of attention. Memories of the fear she had felt when she was presented at Court and had received similar attention flashed through her mind. The words of her aunt, Lady Matlock, came to her suddenly: *Hold your head high and your back straight.*

Straightening her back and raising her head high,

she pasted on a glorious smile and allowed the Duke to lead her into the room.

A man Georgiana had never met came to them and bowed. The Duke smiled and clasped him on the shoulder. "Brother, I am glad you could come tonight. If you will allow me, I would like to introduce you to Miss Darcy and her brother and sister-in-law, Mr. and Mrs. Fitzwilliam Darcy. This is my brother, Lord Carlton Rickords."

"It is a pleasure to meet you all. His Grace has told me much about you." He bowed again and turned back to his brother. "I believe our aunt is expecting you." Lord Rickords looked over his shoulder at the Almack's patronesses, who sat holding court, as it were, at the head of the room.

"Shall we?" the Duke asked Georgiana. He could feel her grip tighten on his arm and gave her a moment to prepare before leading her through the throng of people towards his aunt.

When they stopped in front of Lady Sefton, Georgiana made a deep and gracious curtsey to the woman as the Duke bowed.

"Lady Sefton, it is my honour to present to you Miss Georgiana Darcy of Derbyshire." His voice carried around the ballroom, which had not yet returned to its usual level of noise.

"Ah, Miss Darcy, long have I desired to make your acquaintance. I was speaking with Lady Cowper," she nodded to the lady next to her, who nodded back, "and asking her when she thought you would arrive. If I am not mistaken, she knew your mother, Lady Anne."

"Yes, my lady, you are correct."

"It is very good to see you here, Miss Darcy," Lady Cowper said, "You look a great deal like your mother did at your age. Did your brother come with you?"

"Yes, he and my sister-in-law are standing just there." Georgiana demurely indicated her brother and Elizabeth.

"I don't believe I have met your sister-in-law, though Mrs. Drummond-Burrell tells me she and your brother are very well-suited." Mrs. Drummond-Burrell, seated next to Lady Cowper, nodded in acknowledgement of the truth of Lady Cowper's words. "I shall call them over."

Lady Cowper turned her attention to a footman and directed him to ask Mr. and Mrs. Darcy to attend her. Lady Sefton took the opportunity to dismiss the person next to her and offered the chair to Miss Darcy instead. "If you will, please give me your dance card." Georgiana obeyed, and Lady Sefton handed it to the woman behind her and then proceeded to engage Georgiana in conversation.

For fifteen minutes, Georgiana sat next to Lady Sefton and was the exclusive object of her attention while the Duke stood nearby. At the same time, Lady Cowper entertained Mr. and Mrs. Darcy. When the music began Lady Sefton said, "Your Grace, thank you for allowing me a few minutes of Miss Darcy's time. I apologize for keeping you from your dance. Surely you must not miss it, for Miss Darcy is already engaged for every other dance of the evening."

Lady Sefton returned Georgiana's dance card to her. Every set was taken, and by London's most eligible gentlemen. "Miss Darcy, thank you for accepting my invitation and coming to see me today. You will notice we have also given you permission to dance the waltz."

"Thank you, my lady."

Georgiana stood and offered a departing curtsey as the Duke bowed a second time to his aunt. He then escorted her to the side of the room, Mr. and Mrs. Darcy following close behind.

Chapter Six

Georgiana's entire body was numb and apprehension grew in the pit of her stomach as the Duke guided her to the dance floor. As they assumed the dance position, Georgiana remembered her aunt's words for a second time and stood tall, raising her head proudly. Taking a deep breath, she looked into the face of the Duke. For a moment, she forgot everyone in the room was watching them and got lost in his dark eyes. He was a very handsome man with his raven-black hair and distinctive features.

"Are you ready, Miss Darcy?"

"I am," she replied, and he led her in the first steps of the dance.

Their conversation was neutral, but she couldn't conceal her nervous laugh when she noticed someone being indiscreet and pointing at them.

He responded without missing a beat, turning her away from the gawkers and leading her around the dance floor in another direction. He whirled her around the outer edge of the entire dance floor, making sure everyone saw them together, and at the close of the dance they stopped right in front of his aunt, who deigned to nod in their direction.

At the conclusion of the set, the Duke of Rothford led Georgiana to the Darcys and released her arm. It was not long before her next partner claimed her, and for the rest of the night he was forced to watch as Georgiana was swept up and down the dance floor by the most sought after gentlemen in all of London.

By the end of the night there was not a single person in attendance who still remembered the rumours that a few hours before could not be forgotten. Already news was spreading around the Ton that a grievous error had been made and that Miss Darcy was indeed blameless on all counts.

When it was time to leave, Georgiana and the Darcys stood off to the side while the Duke called for his carriage. Her cheeks were flushed, not only from the exertion of the dance, but also from the Duke's constant regard as his eyes searched her face, taking in every detail. She couldn't help but look at him in return. His eyes were deep, dark pools which she felt in great danger of drowning in, and she savoured the headiness of his masculine sandalwood scent as he helped her on with her cloak.

She was just about to say something to him when she was addressed by one of her dance partners of the evening. "Miss Darcy, it was a pleasure to dance with you tonight. I hope you will allow me to call on you tomorrow?"

Blushing prettily, Georgiana nodded her acceptance.

The gentleman tipped his hat and departed. Georgiana made to speak again, but this time someone rudely cut across her.

"Your Grace, are you going to introduce me to this lady?" an auburn haired beauty said in a too-sweet voice as she stepped in front of them.

"Lady Sophia Beck, what a pleasure it is to see you." Georgiana thought she heard a hint of strain in the Duke's voice. "It is my honour to introduce you to Mr. and Mrs. Fitzwilliam Darcy and Miss Darcy from Derbyshire. And this," he turned to the Darcys, "is Lady Sophia Beck. Her father is the Marquess of Mardsen, my neighbour in Abingdon. His estate abuts the Rothford duchy."

The Darcys greeted Lady Sophia politely with bows and curtsies. Georgiana was still holding the Duke's arm. Lady Sophia noticed and raised a delicate eyebrow.

"Your Grace, I had not realized you had returned to London. I thought I understood from my father that you were due home earlier this week."

"I was in Abingdon but a day before urgent business called me back. I sent word to your father that our meeting would be delayed."

"I see. I'm sure your time in London has been well spent and my father will not resent you for the delay." Her words were kind, but Georgiana could hear the hint of a threat behind them. "Well, I shall leave you all; my carriage has just been called. It was a pleasure to make your acquaintance. Goodbye." Georgiana could feel the Duke's sigh of relief when Lady Sophia excused herself and rushed off in a swirl of fabric and lace.

Georgiana wondered what Lady Sophia meant by her words, but of course held her tongue.

At last their carriage was announced and the Duke handed in Georgiana first and then allowed her siblings to follow. As soon as the carriage moved away from the kerb, Georgiana let out a deep sigh which no one failed to notice.

"If you will allow me to speak freely," the Duke said, "I think this evening was a resounding success. I predict we will be free from any future rumours and our lives may very well return to normal by Friday."

"Do you really think so?" Georgiana asked, afraid his view was too optimistic.

"I think you will be surprised how soon the scandal will be forgotten now that Lady Sefton, Lady Cowper, and Mrs. Drummond-Brunnell have accepted your society. Do you not agree, Mr. Darcy?"

"I do agree. Georgiana, you should be able to finish out the season without fear of being shunned. It is amazing how short a memory the Ton has in these cases. And nothing speeds forgetfulness faster than the acceptance of the Almack's patronesses."

"I hope so." Georgiana's voice was full of emotion. "Before we cancel our plans to return to Pemberley I would like to see how widespread the news of tonight travels. If it is as you say, I would not be opposed to remaining in London."

As the Duke's carriage neared the Darcys' townhouse Fitzwilliam said, "Your Grace, thank you for your kind invitation and the extraordinary lengths you went to in order to recover Miss Darcy's reputation. I shall forever be indebted to you."

"You are too kind, Mr. Darcy. Although the circumstances were not ideal, I am honoured I have made your family's acquaintance."

"Thank you, Your Grace, the honour is all ours," Fitzwilliam responded humbly.

"I will repeat my request from earlier; I hope you will allow me to call again. I want to be certain Miss Darcy suffers no lasting ill effects from these unfortunate circumstances."

"It would be our honour to receive you at any time."

When the carriage door was opened by a liveried footman, Fitzwilliam stepped out and offered his hand to Elizabeth and Georgiana. The Duke remained in his carriage.

"Until we meet again," he called as the carriage departed.

Georgiana collapsed on the drawing room settee. Elizabeth took her seat nearby and accepted the glass of wine Fitzwilliam offered her.

"Georgie, why don't you have some wine? It should help calm your nerves," Fitzwilliam said, offering her a glass as well.

"Thank you, brother." Georgiana accepted the

glass, taking a small sip. "I could not have expected half the success we had tonight. We knew Lady Sefton would accept our society, but I had no notion that Lady Cowper and Mrs. Drummond-Brunnell would as well. It was very kind of them to include you. In my haste to repair my own reputation I almost forgot this has had damaging effects on both of you."

"Fear not for us," Elizabeth said. "Your brother and I were never worried for ourselves. We have only been worried for you. I am glad we now have something good to rejoice in."

"Yes," Georgiana said fervently. "As am I."

Despite her desperate need for decent rest after so many nights of worrying and tears, Georgiana did not think she would sleep much that night. Her head was far too full of her successful evening and the hope that in the following days she would be able to leave the house without the threat of scandal following in her wake.

Chapter Seven

Less than two weeks had passed since the rumours began to spread, and for the first time since then Georgiana did not fear the day when she opened her eyes.

She had taken particular care with her appearance this morning just in case the Duke or anyone else came to call. After her rose-scented bath, her hair was dried, brushed, twisted, and piled high on her head with bright ribbons. The mauve visiting dress Mary helped her into brought out the ivory glow of her flawless complexion.

No one had come to visit them recently, except Elizabeth's aunt, but after Wednesday's display at Almack's visitors and well-wishers flooded the Darcys' doorstep. Never had they received so many visitors at the townhouse in a single day. It was testament to their success of the previous night. Georgiana wasn't sure she was equal to entertaining stranger after stranger, but after the fourth caller had left Elizabeth assured her she was putting on a spectacular performance.

Georgiana expected that if the Duke did visit it would be soon. Indeed, it wasn't long before Mr. Grey announced the gentleman. "His Grace the Duke of Rothford."

"Please show him in," Elizabeth said with what Georgiana thought was remarkable calm, as if her sister-in-law received peers of the realm in her sitting room every day.

Once again, the Duke strode into the sitting room with all the confidence in the world. Georgiana wondered how it was not somehow illegal to look as handsome as he did. Today he wore dark pantaloons and a matching overcoat. His white starched shirt and intricately tied cravat were perfectly set off by his red brocade waistcoat.

When she had first met him she had been taken with how handsome he was, but now, with the sun streaming through the window and London gossips far from her mind, his many good attributes seemed magnified. He was mighty, a specimen of raw and manly power. He was incomparable to every other man of her acquaintance.

"Good morning, Miss Darcy." He stopped in front of her and bowed, as he looked deep into her eyes. Turning to Elizabeth, he addressed her too, giving Georgiana a little time to recover from the tingling sensations settling around her heart. "Mrs. Darcy, it is good to see you this morning."

"Thank you, Your Grace. We are pleased you could visit with us today."

"Would you like a cup of tea?" Georgiana offered. "Just milk, if I remember correctly."

He nodded and accepted the cup of tea. He noticed how Georgiana's hands slightly trembled as she handed it to him.

"It is lovely weather we are having, isn't it?" Georgiana observed in an effort to start the conversation.

"Yes, yes it is," the Duke was quick to agree, "though a little colder than usual. Have you enjoyed your time in London?" He raised his cup and sipped his tea. A shadow crossed over Georgiana's face and instantly he realised his mistake. "Miss Darcy, I am so sorry. I was not thinking."

"It is nothing." Georgiana schooled her expression behind her tea cup and then continued. "How is it that scandal can make the most mundane conversational topics taboo?"

"It is most vexing. I hardly know what topics of conversation are safe."

"I doubt anything is safe."

"You may very well be correct. Rather than avoid the topics, we shall attack them with a frontal assault."

Georgiana smiled at his zeal. "Very well, Your Grace, what topic do you propose?"

"Let me see." He pretended he was thinking, cupping his jaw between his thumb and finger, and said, "Well, if the number of visitors and cards presented at your door is even a fraction of the number at mine, I shall hazard a guess that last night's performance was a resounding success. I must have received ten callers already this morning."

"I would have to agree with you, for we have received a bevy of callers also. More than we have ever received in a single day prior to this."

"A bevy, you say. Pray tell, how many callers does it take to make a bevy?" His grin was rather impish as he set his tea aside and reclined in his seat.

"You are the fifth gentleman to grace the sitting room today, and Mr. Grey has informed us that another three have sent their cards."

"Eight! I never would have imagined so many," he drolled.

Georgiana knew she was being teased but knew not how to respond. Elizabeth teased her frequently in a charming and sisterly way, but she was not used to receiving the same from a gentleman. Therefore she was entirely honest in her reply when she said, "Nor I. I am sure it is only to see what made Lady Sefton speak to me for a full quarter of an hour."

"I think you underestimate your own charms, Miss Darcy."

A pretty blush crept up Georgiana's neck and settled on her cheeks. She could scarcely look at him, so embarrassed was she.

They sat in silence while they all sipped their tea. Elizabeth gave Georgiana time to compose herself and then urged her with a look to say something more. She gathered her courage and said, "My brother informed me your father recently passed. Please allow me to offer my sincerest condolences at this time. I am so sorry you have been made to deal with these distressing rumours at a time when you should be allowed peace to mourn his passing."

"You are very thoughtful, Miss Darcy, but my father died a little more than six months ago. I was provided ample time to mourn prior to this. I can honestly say the worst of my sorrow is behind me and that I have been able to once again find joy in many of my favourite pursuits. I do thank you for your kind words, however."

"And what kind of pursuits do you find enjoyable?" Georgiana asked with sincere interest.

"Oh, the usual gentlemanly pastimes: riding, hunting, fishing, those sorts of things. What about you? What pastimes do you enjoy?"

Under Elizabeth's encouraging gaze, Georgiana spoke of her passion for music and art, and her love of long walks and phaeton rides on Pemberley's extensive grounds.

"Those are admirable pastimes for any lady," the Duke declared. "Perhaps one day I will have the pleasure of hearing you play. Your brother has told me what an accomplished pianist you are."

"I would be happy to play for you one day, Your Grace."

Now that they had broken the ice their conversation flowed much easier. The Duke regaled the ladies with stories of growing up at Rothrage Castle near Abingdon. In turn, Georgiana spoke of Pemberley and the beautiful scenery in Derbyshire. She described the beauty of the Peaks with such feeling that the Duke expressed a genuine wish to see them.

"I have some drawings of the place if you would like to see them."

The Duke's countenance brightened. "Yes, I would like that very much."

Georgiana fetched her portfolio and handed him a sketch of the Peaks. She watched his face anxiously as he studied it. She rarely shared her drawings with anyone outside of her family.

"Beautiful!" the Duke said as he inspected every inch of the drawing. "I feel as if I am there, as if I am standing on the precipice with you."

"That is one of my favourite views." She pointed at the picture. "There is a little road over here that runs back this way. Mr. Darcy has often brought me here. It was one of my mother's favourite places. I feel close to her when I am there. I have another from the same place." She pulled a second drawing from the portfolio and placed it beside the first. "This view is from the other direction. See this spot right here?" She pointed at the image once more. "You can see it is on the other picture as well."

"I see; they create a panorama." He inspected the second image as intently as he had the first. "Miss Darcy, these are breathtaking. You have a wonderful talent."

A pink hue overspread her features as she replaced the drawings in her portfolio and laid it aside.

Mr. Grey entered at that time to announce the arrival of a Mr. Bushman to see Miss Darcy. "What message would you like me to give him, madam?"

Elizabeth was about to speak when the Duke stood

to leave.

"It has been my pleasure to sit with you today. I shall not detain you from your other admirers." Georgiana would have thought his words a joke if she hadn't noticed a flicker of insecurity in his generally confident expression. "I hope you will allow me to visit you again."

"I would like that," Georgiana said as she and Elizabeth returned his farewell bow with curtseys.

He paused at the door and said, "Mrs. Darcy, if you have no fixed engagements for tomorrow evening, I should like to invite yourself and Mr. Darcy, and of course Miss Darcy, to the theatre tomorrow night."

Elizabeth smiled at the Duke. "You honour us, Your Grace. We gladly accept your invitation."

"I am happy to hear it. I will call for you at six."

"We shall look forward to it," Georgiana said as he retired from the room and Mr. Grey showed in Mr. Bushman.

Georgiana was standing near the window and happened to glance out to see the Duke accept the reins of a white gelding. Her hand flew to her throat and she caught her breath as he put one foot in the stirrup and gracefully swung onto the back of the magnificent animal. Settling into the saddle, he kicked his horse's sides and moved out of sight. Georgiana turned away from the window and tried to pay attention during Mr. Bushman's visit, but truth be told, all she could think about was the Duke of Rothford and his white horse. Might he be the white knight her cousin had promised her?

Chapter Eight

"Elizabeth, do you believe in destiny?" Georgiana asked as soon as Mr. Bushman departed and the sitting room door closed behind him.

"I do, in a sense." Elizabeth set aside her book, which she had just picked up. "If by destiny you mean something is supposed to happen, then yes I do believe in it. I differ from most in that I believe destiny forms due to cause and effect, not because our course is set from the beginning. Call it coincidence, destiny, or fate, I believe that in one moment lives can collide and change forever. I believe you can make your own destiny by opening yourself to the world."

"That makes sense." Georgiana thought for a moment and then asked, "Do you also believe we reap what we sow?"

"I do, in the same sense as destiny. I think you reap the rewards and consequences of your own actions. People who strive to be good generally associate with good people and therefore will be happy and have a good life. Those who are evil generally associate with others who are evil. Those people tend to do more harm than good to one another; therefore, they open themselves up to be hurt throughout their life."

"That is just what I think," Georgiana said. "I shall look at the past fortnight as a positive thing. Someone evil tried to hurt me, but in the end, they will not succeed. I choose to make the most of it."

"I am glad you take this view of things. Your brother and I have been so worried for you."

"You are both so kind to me." Georgiana clasped Elizabeth's hand in her own. "Lizzy, I am glad you are my sister."

"As am I, dearest. Now, what do you say to a bit of shopping today? I am dying to get out of this house and your brother has said we may go out."

"I would like that. When shall we go?"

Elizabeth looked at the clock on the mantle. "The time for morning calls has passed. We may leave as soon as we are ready. Shall we say an hour?"

Georgiana agreed, and the two ladies walked arm-in-arm up the grand staircase. Before parting ways to go to their separate rooms, Georgiana stopped and said, "Oh, I almost forgot to tell you. When His Grace left the house I looked out the window and saw his horse. What do you think, Elizabeth? He rides a white horse. A pure white horse!"

Elizabeth laughed. "Does he indeed? All he needs now is a suit of armour."

"I think that may be asking a little too much, though he did say there are several on display at

Rothrage Castle."

Elizabeth laughed again and then adopted a more sober tone. "Georgiana, you should not get your hopes up," she cautioned in all seriousness. "His Grace is not likely to ever consider you as a marriage prospect. I do not want to pain you, but I am sure his attendance on you is only a result of the remorse he feels because of the scandalous rumours levelled at you in connection with himself."

A shadow of pain crossed Georgiana's face. "I know, Elizabeth, but I shall enjoy his company while he continues to offer it."

"Very well, so long as you remember what I said and have no expectations regarding the Duke's affections. Now, run along and get dressed. We leave in an hour."

*J*ust over an hour later, Georgiana was looking out the carriage window as they approached Mayfair. The streets were bustling despite the cold weather.

"Lizzy, is that Richard?" Georgiana asked, indicating a man half hidden in the shadows of a narrow alley.

Elizabeth tried to make out the man's features before the carriage passed the alley. "I'm not sure, but I'm inclined to think not."

"Yes, I'm sure it is him." Georgiana craned her neck to see again, but the man was out of sight.

"Why would Richard be skulking around in the shadows of Mayfair?"

"I don't know. Perhaps he is on a military assignment. It did seem as if he was watching the carriages."

"Military assignments in the shopping district?" Elizabeth cocked her head to the side, her eyes sparkling with amusement. "What, is he here to defend London from subversive French fashions?"

"No, I suppose you are right," Georgiana conceded with a laugh, though she couldn't help but wonder. She had been so sure it was her cousin.

"*Lizzy*! Georgiana!" called the high-pitched voice of Lydia Wickham as they alighted from the carriage in front of the bookshop.

Lydia stood across the street with a small group of women and officers. She was waving madly and bobbing like a rowdy child to get their attention.

Elizabeth nodded to her, but went no further to acknowledge her and made no effort to go to her.

Lydia lifted her skirts indecently high and ran across the street towards them, dodging carriages and men on horseback.

"Lydia, what were you thinking?" Elizabeth scolded when Lydia reached the sidewalk and nearly bowled her over in her enthusiasm.

"Whatever do you mean? Did you not see me, Lizzy? I called to you and waved."

"We saw you, Lydia. Did you not see me nod to you?"

"La! Lizzy, how silly you are. I am your sister;

you cannot just nod to me and go about your business. Are you not surprised to see me? What about you, Georgiana? It has been an age since we met. Last time I saw you was a year after my wedding. To think, I have been married more than four years already. Who would have thought time could fly so quickly?"

"We are happy to see you, Lydia." Elizabeth maintained a genuine interest in her sister's comings and goings despite the fact that, more often than not, Lydia's tales of her exploits were mortifying. "I did not know you were in London." Elizabeth looked back across the street to the group of people still standing there. "Is Mr. Wickham not with you?"

"Of course he is. Fancy me coming to London by myself!" Lydia snorted in laughter. "He was here a moment ago. He let me off just over there." She pointed to a spot down the street. "He has some business or other and I refused to sit at our lodgings waiting for him, so I arranged to meet with some friends to go shopping. I am in desperate need of a new parasol." She rolled her eyes heavenward. "Lord, how boring he has become. Every day he has someone he must meet or somewhere he must be. If it was up to him I would be left in my room to shift for myself all day, but I will not have it. I have plenty of friends to keep me company."

"Lydia, I'm afraid your friends are leaving you." Elizabeth indicated her sister's companions, who were beginning to move away. "Perhaps you had better join them."

Waving at them to go on without her, Lydia

returned her attention to Elizabeth and said, "I should much rather come with you. I haven't had a chance to tell you my news yet."

She cheerfully linked her arm through Elizabeth's, giving her no other choice but to bring Lydia into the shop with them.

"Good day, Mr. Cooper," Georgiana greeted the shopkeeper.

"Hello, Miss Darcy. How good it is to see you today. Mrs. Darcy." He bowed his head and motioned for her to come to the counter. "You have come at just the right time. I have two new books I am certain you will enjoy."

While Elizabeth spoke with Mr. Cooper and Lydia fidgeted impatiently at her side, Georgiana perused the books, walking up and down the length of the shelves and running her finger along the leather spines.

She loved everything about books. She loved the smell of them. She loved the look of them all lined up with their spines facing out in neat rows of lettering. She loved to open them and gently fan the paper. Most of all, she loved to get lost in their pages.

After selecting a book of poetry, she went to Elizabeth and Lydia and told them she was ready to leave.

Elizabeth, clearly out of patience with Lydia, paid for their purchases and accepted the wrapped package of books from Mr. Cooper, handing them to the footman to load into the carriage.

Leaving the warmth and comfort of the bookshop, they returned to the cold and busy street beyond.

"It was nice to see you, Lydia," Elizabeth said, offering her a kiss on each cheek. "We must be going now."

"But, Lizzy, you did not yet hear my news. I will tell you in the carriage. Can you not take me to meet my husband? It is too far to walk and I don't have any money to hire a chair."

"I thought you told us Mr. Wickham was nearby," Elizabeth said mildly.

"He is. It is only a mile and a half to Regent's Park is it not?"

"It is. A mile and a half is an easy distance to walk. Why, I've walked twice as far and in the country. The paved paths of London will make such a walk seem as nothing."

"But, Lizzy, if I walk I shall be too late. He expects me to find my way back to our lodgings with my friends. If you do not take me to the park to meet him then I shall likely miss him and need to be taken to our lodgings."

"Where are you lodgings?" Elizabeth asked.

"In the Port District. My dear Wicky knows a woman who lets us rooms for very little."

Georgiana and Elizabeth looked at one another. They both knew who the lady must be, and neither of them had any intention of going to the Port District.

"Regent's Park is too far out of our way and the Port District is out of the question. What if I give you money for a chair?"

"Why cannot you take me yourself? A mere mile and a half cannot be so far out of your way." Lydia stamped her foot. "I thought you would care more for me. I am your sister after all."

Georgiana thought she saw Elizabeth roll her eyes to the heavens again.

"Very well, get in."

The air in the carriage was thick with the pent-up tension between Elizabeth and Lydia. Elizabeth had no love for her sister's husband and would have rather avoided a meeting with him. Georgiana was perhaps even less eager than she, and the tension was unbearable. She sought to ease the strain with some conversation.

"Lydia, you mentioned you had some news?"

"I do! It is matters pertaining to this news that sent my husband to the Inner Circle of Regent's Park on business. Can you believe it? My dear Wicky and I will be moving to Abingdon." Georgiana couldn't believe it. In fact, her jaw dropped open involuntarily. "I can see you are surprised. Isn't it wonderful? Wicky has a friend who is looking for a new steward to manage his large estate. You know, my dear Wicky's father was a steward. I am certain he will be excellent in his new position."

After a moment of silence Georgiana was finally able to stutter her congratulations, her face draining of colour. "I am very happy for you."

"I am sure you are." Lydia giggled and looked out the window. "Lizzy, can you believe our good fortune? We are to take a house. We travel to Abingdon by the middle of next week. No more of the horrible military lodgings we've been forced to suffer in the past four years."

Lydia babbled on about Wickham and his new position while they made their way through the busy streets of London to Regent's Park. She cared not that Elizabeth and Georgiana failed to respond to her. By the time they arrived, Elizabeth was sure her sister could have walked the mile and a half from Mayfair to Regent's Park in half the time.

Georgiana and Elizabeth both sighed with relief when the carriage came to a stop and the footman threw open the door and pulled down the stairs.

Lydia alighted without assistance, disregarding the footman's outstretched hand, and then stood at the carriage door to say her farewells. "My Wicky will be so jealous when he hears I rode in one of the fine Darcy carriages. Goodbye, Lizzy! Goodbye, Georgiana! Wait, here's George now. I'm sure he will want to say hello."

"It's all right, Lydia, we really must be going," Elizabeth said, trying to avoid the dreaded meeting.

"Nonsense! He is your brother, after all." Lydia remained where she was, preventing the footman from closing the door, and called out, "Wicky, come say hello to my sister."

Through the open door, Georgiana and Elizabeth could just see Captain Wickham standing with his back to them, speaking with another officer and a lady a little ways off. Wickham had startled slightly at the unexpected sound of Lydia's voice. When he turned around, Georgiana got her first clear glimpse of his companions. She gasped at the sight of Lady Sophia Beck and a young man who bore a strong family resemblance, perhaps a brother or cousin. She sank back into her seat so she would not be seen.

"Do not let him distress you, dearest," Elizabeth murmured, misinterpreting Georgiana's behaviour.

"I am well, Elizabeth. I was just surprised to see Lady Sophia Beck."

"What? Here? Speaking to Wickham? Is that not most unusual?" Elizabeth tried to see beyond Lydia, who was bobbing up and down with her usual exuberance. "Wait, here he comes. We shall talk about this later."

Lady Sophia and her companion had disappeared down the line of carriages by then, and Wickham sauntered over, oozing false charm and cooing greetings to his wife.

"Lydia, dear, what are you doing here?"

"La, Wicky, look who I ran into in Mayfair. I left my friends to visit with my dear sister, so we had no other choice but for her to bring me to you."

Leaning against the carriage, Captain Wickham peered through the door. "Hello, Mrs. Darcy, Miss Darcy." Georgiana and Elizabeth nodded in greeting. "Thank you for returning my dear Lydia to me. I am most obliged to you."

"You are welcome, sir," Elizabeth replied. "Now, if you will excuse us, we must be going." Without waiting for their reply, she said, "John, the door."

Lydia had to jump out of the way when the footman stepped forward and began closing the door even though he was in danger of crushing her skirts. Georgiana clearly heard Lydia curse the man.

Normally she would have been shocked by a lady using such vulgar language, but she had learned not to be shocked by anything Lydia Wickham said or did. She had never been so relieved as when she felt the carriage pull away from the kerb.

She had just let out a deep sigh of relief when she felt the carriage bounce, almost as if another footman had jumped on the back.

"Elizabeth …" Georgiana's voice was shaky.

"I know, I felt him too."

"Do you think it is Captain Wickham?"

"Surely not. Whoever it is, John will take care of it." Her words were confident, but the tremor in her voice betrayed her.

Georgiana and Elizabeth sat close, frequently looking at one another in concern. A moment later, the carriage slowed and the man jumped off. Just when they were beginning to wonder what was going on, the carriage door flung open and a man dressed in a military uniform stepped in as the carriage moved forward again.

Georgiana cried out, "Merciful God, help us," as Elizabeth assailed the man with her reticule.

"Elizabeth! Georgiana! It is me, Richard. Calm yourselves."

Georgiana crumbled and burst into tears and Elizabeth halted her assault, demanding an explanation for why and how he had appeared in their carriage like a brigand a few streets from Regent's Park.

"I was following Captain Wickham to ascertain what he is doing in town, and what do I find but the two of you playing escort to his wife. What was she doing with you?"

"We met by chance in Mayfair. I did not even know they were in London until we encountered her outside the bookshop."

"I am sure you did not since he has tried to keep their whereabouts secret. He claims he is on leave from his regiment, but I have received word he may have deserted his position and I am determined to discover the truth."

"Why were Lady Sophia Beck and that other officer speaking with him?" Georgiana asked when she was finally in control of her emotions.

"You know them?" Richard asked in surprise.

"We were introduced to Lady Sophia at Almack's yesterday. I can only assume the officer with her was a family member, though I have never met any of them."

"Who introduced you?" Richard's voice had become stern and demanding.

"The Duke of Rothford. Lord Mardsen's estate abuts the Duke's duchy near Abingdon."

"What else do you know?"

"Why do you ask?"

"Simply because I had planned on following their carriage to learn more about them, but when I noticed the two of you I came after you instead. I am sure Fitzwilliam would never forgive me if he knew I saw you anywhere near Captain Wickham and did not escort you home."

"We are not going directly home," Elizabeth said.

"We plan to return to our shopping. We have been kept indoors far too long and need a little time away."

"I am afraid I have already directed the driver to return to your townhouse. Perhaps you will consent to go there and let me out before returning to your errands?"

"If you've already instructed the driver of the change, we have very little to say in the matter."

"Touché. Now, tell me what you know and then I will leave you in peace to spend my cousin's money."

"We do not know much else, Richard," Georgiana said. "After all, we have only met her once. I will say this, though: when we met her, it was not all pleasant. I had the feeling she was levelling a threat at the Duke, and when she departed he was very happy to see her go. What about you, Elizabeth? Did you feel the same way?"

"Indeed I did. In all honesty, I wondered if I was the only one who thought their greeting was very cold despite their familiar manner with one another. I also thought the Duke was very happy to see her leave."

"Interesting," Richard said. "Is that all?"

Georgiana and Elizabeth nodded. When they arrived at the townhouse, Richard said, "You ladies have a lovely time shopping. I shall report to my cousin and do a little more investigating."

Elizabeth forestalled him. "Richard, will you stay for dinner tonight? I should like to hear everything you've discovered."

"Yes, I would like that." The carriage door opened and Richard jumped out. Before closing the door, he said, "Georgie, I am very glad to hear the tittle-tattle around town seems to have magically disappeared overnight. I shall look forward to hearing your version of the ball at Almack's, though I have heard of the events from at least five individuals already."

"As you can well imagine, I am very happy it seems to be over."

"Let us pray your good fortune holds." Richard closed the carriage door and directed the driver to take Elizabeth and Georgiana to their original destination.

It did not take long for the carriage to arrive at the Bond Street Chocolatiere. The delicious gourmet sweets and hot chocolate were just what the women needed to brighten the gloom that had descended upon them since the gossip had set in around London.

While Elizabeth was selecting an assortment of sweets to take home with them, Georgiana stayed at their table to finish her chocolates. The bell at the front of the shop jingled occasionally as patrons arrived or departed, but Georgiana never looked up until she heard a silky smooth voice address her directly.

"Why, it is Miss Darcy! What a pleasure it is to see you here."

Georgiana closed her eyes briefly before turning to face Lady Sophia Beck. It was only their second meeting, but the lady caused her uneasiness, especially after discovering she had some sort of connection with Captain Wickham.

"Good afternoon, Lady Sophia," Georgiana said as she quickly stood and curtsied, a pasted smile on her face. "How good it is to see you again." Georgiana responded as politeness dictated, though she felt a trifle duplicitous knowing she didn't mean the words.

"It has always amazed me how two people can so frequently see one another around town once they have been introduced. Why, we've probably passed each other on the street a dozen times and not realized it."

"London is deceptively small." Georgiana willed Elizabeth to return and rescue her, but she was still selecting chocolates and had not even noticed Lady Sophia's arrival. "Please, sit down." Georgiana indicated the seat next to her at the table.

"Thank you, I will." Lady Sophia sat on the edge of the chair and adjusted her skirts. "I must say, I was surprised to see you with the Duke of Rothford at Almack's last night. He had an appointment with my father in Abingdon this week, but my father was forced to come to London instead."

"I'm sorry, I am not privy to His Grace's business dealings. Perhaps we should discuss something with which we are both familiar? How are you enjoying the season?" Georgiana asked, trying to remain cheerful and calm.

"I was greatly enjoying it until recently," Lady Sophia replied, leaning back in her seat and staring at Georgiana.

"I'm sorry to hear it. Perhaps your luck will change. Many believe that once March arrives London vastly improves." Once again, Georgiana looked for Elizabeth. It could not possibly take this long to select a few chocolates.

Lady Sophia was clearly trying to unnerve her with her piercing gaze. "Yes, well, we shall see. My father is in town to make sure the Duke pays his debts, and once that disagreeable business is taken care of I shall be right as rain. My father has promised me a summer in Bath and I am very much looking forward to going there while he inspects his new estate."

Georgiana was surprised at Lady Sophia's crassness. To air someone's private affairs in a public place was very indiscreet.

"Oh dear, I can see I have said too much and shocked you. Please forget I said it. The Duke would not be pleased if he knew I told you he gambled away one of his estates to my father. Drat, there I go again opening my big mouth. Perhaps I had better take my leave before I tell any more of the family's dark business."

Without so much as a goodbye, Lady Sophia stood and walked away, leaving Georgiana stunned. As she paused nearby to speak with someone else, Lady Sophia's sinister eyes kept darting back to Georgiana.

"Georgiana, are you all right?" Elizabeth said, resuming her seat with her purchase in hand.

"I should like very much to go home now." Georgiana stood quickly, putting on her cloak and nodding at John, who rushed outside and waved the driver to bring the carriage around.

Elizabeth studied her pale face and shaking hands, and then rose to put on her own outerwear. "Very well. Home it is."

When John returned to announce the Darcy

carriage, Georgiana rushed out of the shop, not caring whether Elizabeth followed or not.

Georgiana was already seated and staring out the window when Elizabeth took her seat. As the carriage began to move, Elizabeth leaned over to touch Georgiana's knee. "Dearest, you must tell me what this fuss is about. What happened while I was picking out chocolates?"

"I spoke with Lady Sophia Beck."

"She was there? I did not see her."

"Yes, she was there. She accosted me while you were at the counter and revealed some very private business of the Duke of Rothford's—business no one but those he chooses to trust ought to know about."

"I think you should tell your brother."

"Yes, I think I must. I am certain the Duke will want to know how Lady Sophia is maligning his good name in public. I am sure others in the shop could hear her."

When the carriage arrived home, Elizabeth and Georgiana found Fitzwilliam in the library with Richard. When Georgiana related Lady Sophia's indiscreet revelations, he knew what he must do.

"I must go to His Grace immediately," Fitzwilliam said. "Richard, will you come with me?"

"Yes. I would like to ask the Duke a few questions myself. Perhaps he has some additional information which will help me discover why Mr. Wickham has come to London and was speaking with the Marquess's daughter."

Elizabeth exchanged glances with Georgiana

and said, "Lydia told us her husband is accepting the position of steward at a large estate in Abingdon. Is it possible his prospective employer is the Marquess?"

"It certainly looks that way," Richard said. "Why did you not tell me this before?"

"We might have done, had you not frightened us out of our wits."

Richard took his scolding good-naturedly and departed with Fitzwilliam. Georgiana excused herself and went to her rooms. As soon as the door closed behind her, she threw herself upon her bed and cried. She marvelled at the power Lady Sophia seemed to have over her. Never had another person so wholly unconnected with her upset her in such a way.

Chapter Nine

Since Lady Sophia had revealed the Duke of Rothford's personal matters yesterday, Georgiana had done nothing but worry about him. She had a sneaking suspicion there was more to the situation than the lady had disclosed. She clearly had sinister motives. Georgiana knew the Duke was more than capable of taking care of himself and his business dealings, but she was concerned for him all the same. He had done much for her these past weeks, and though she knew she had no hope of his ever returning her feelings, she could not deny she had begun to have them.

Georgiana sat on the edge of her bed and tried to compose herself. The Duke would be there soon to escort them to the theatre. She hated that Lady Sophia had the power to distress her so. Taking a deep, cleansing breath, she squared her shoulders and stood, ready to face the whole of London.

"His Grace the Duke of Rothford has arrived," Georgiana heard Mr. Grey announce as she descended the stairs. The Duke stood with his back to her in the foyer. He turned at the sound of her mules clicking against the stairs.

"Good evening, Miss Darcy," the Duke said, bowing.

"Good evening, Your Grace."

Fitzwilliam and Elizabeth came out of the sitting room and met them in the foyer.

"My driver tells me the streets are full tonight. We should leave right away to make sure we are on time," the Duke said to Fitzwilliam.

"Very well, let us be off." Fitzwilliam helped Elizabeth with her wrap while the Duke took the opportunity to assist Georgiana.

When Mr. Grey opened the door for them, she once again stepped into the cool night air on the Duke's arm and breathed in his heady scent. For a moment, she considered that given the chance she would be happy to smell his masculine scent for the rest of her life.

"The colour of your gown suits you, Miss Darcy," the Duke said once they were all seated in his carriage. "I like it very much."

"Thank you, Your Grace."

"I hope your steady stream of callers did not diminish after I departed yesterday." That mischievous sparkle was back in his eyes. Georgiana was astonished at his ability to jest in so carefree a manner when his neighbour was apparently bent on ruining him. She reasoned that the situation must not be so terrible after all, and she strove to match his playful mood.

"I believe another score of gentlemen came to our door. Isn't that right, Elizabeth?"

"Yes, dearest, I believe you are correct. Mr. Grey told me they were queued up around the block, waiting for the chance to sit with you for five minutes."

"Five minutes!" the Duke exclaimed. "The poor souls. I must have been privileged indeed, for I sat with you for three times that."

"You were indeed very lucky." Georgiana laughed, making Fitzwilliam and Elizabeth smile. It had been far too long since she had laughed like that. "In all seriousness, Mr. Bushman, who arrived as you were leaving, was the final caller of the day. After he left, Mrs. Darcy and I went shopping. We were very glad to leave the house after so many days confined indoors."

They continued to chat about trivial matters until the carriage turned onto Drury Lane. Dusk had already descended upon the streets and the Lamplighters were at their work atop their ladders. The lights twinkled and winked and brought the city nightlife alive.

Georgiana watched a variety of people heading towards the theatre. Gentlemen and ladies walked arm in arm looking elegant in their evening attire. Members of the working class enjoying a much-needed night off were also making their way to the theatre, as well as a party of ladies vying for the attention of several militiamen who loitered on the street corner.

"Elizabeth, is that Lydia?" Georgiana asked, pointing discreetly out the window.

"Oh dear, I believe it is," Elizabeth said with a sigh.

"What is the matter? Who is Lydia?" the Duke pressed.

"She is Mrs. Darcy's youngest sister; she is married to a Captain Wickham, who is stationed in Newcastle. Our cousin oversees his commission," Georgiana explained.

"Is her husband the man we spoke of?" the Duke asked Mr. Darcy.

"He is."

When their carriage came to a stop, the footman opened the door and the gentlemen stepped out first. The Duke handed out Georgiana and then Fitzwilliam handed out Elizabeth. The ladies were shaking out their skirts when Lydia caught sight of them.

"Lizzy! Lizzy!" The high-pitched sound of Lydia's voice rose above all the commotion on the street and drew everyone's attention. Lydia came rushing over and stepped into the midst of their party uninvited. "La, what a funny thing seeing you here. I never imagined I would see you so many times by accident."

Elizabeth clasped Lydia's hands and kissed her cheek. "Is Captain Wickham with you tonight?"

"No, he had business again. He is becoming such a bore, Lizzy! He never takes me out anymore so I go without him. These are some of our friends." Lydia threw a look over her shoulder at the group of people behind them.

Elizabeth curtsied to the group who returned the

gesture, their manners clearly more refined than her sister's.

"Hello, Georgiana. Can you believe we are meeting like this again? And who is this?" she continued before Georgiana could answer. She eyed the Duke of Rothford openly, the smile on her face approaching a leer.

"Lydia," hissed Elizabeth, "you do not seek introductions to people who are clearly your superiors. Excuse me, Your Grace, I must apologize for my—"

The Duke raised his hand to silence Elizabeth. "I am the Duke of Rothford. Now, if you will excuse us, we really must make our way to our seats. I despise being late to the opening."

His dismissal of Lydia was clear, as he neither asked her name nor expressed any pleasure at their meeting. The Duke gently guided Georgiana up the stairs, leaving the Darcys to deal with Lydia.

Georgiana was horrified when she heard Lydia loudly exclaim, "How dreadful he is! I shouldn't like to be Georgiana, forced to parade around London with him just because her name was linked with his in so many scandals. Don't look as if you don't know, Lizzy. It's all over town. Oh well, I guess if she must go around with the man it is a fine thing he is a duke. I wish my Wicky were a duke. Could you imagine? What fun that would be."

Georgiana felt the Duke stiffen and halt. He turned around and glared at Lydia with narrowed eyes. Gently and purposefully, he guided Georgiana back to Mr. and Mrs. Darcy, who were already scolding

Lydia for her thoughtless outburst. The group fell silent when the Duke approached. Fear rose up in Georgiana. In an irrational moment, she was afraid Lydia's performance would prompt him to leave her right there on the street in front of Drury Lane, causing rumours to flare up all over again.

Taking a deep breath, the Duke of Rothford stood tall and imposing in front of Lydia. "Mrs. Wickham, I would ask that you never say such things in my presence ever again. Miss Darcy is a pure and innocent woman who has been the victim of vicious and mendacious gossip bandied about London by those too ignorant to seek the truth. You may think and say what you will about me, but you will never speak so of Miss Darcy again. Is that understood?"

Georgiana's admiration for the Duke increased despite Elizabeth's cautions and her own understanding that she should not allow her heart to become attached to him.

Not waiting for Lydia's reply, he turned away from her, leading Georgiana up the stairs. Mr. and Mrs. Darcy followed, leaving a gaping Lydia standing alone on the sidewalk. Her so-called friends had abandoned her as soon as the Duke's scolding began.

He helped Georgiana remove her cloak in the coat room and then leaned close to whisper, "You are not distressed by what happened outside, are you?"

She shivered as his breath caressed her ear. "I am well, thank you." He took her shawl from her hands, shook it out, and wrapped it around her shoulders, allowing his hands to lightly rest on her arms for a fraction of a second. Her skin heated under his hands and she looked   down at her shoes peeking out from under the hem of her gown, afraid to meet his gaze.

"Hold your head high, Miss Darcy," the Duke insisted. "You look down to no one."

Everyone and everything faded around her until it was just the two of them standing there. She longed for him to want more from her, but she knew she was being irrational. He would not. Was it even possible? Could a man in his position ever love a woman of her station?

Georgiana had never in her life been made to feel inferior to anyone. She had grown up with the Darcy wealth and her brother had never denied her anything. She had never desired status or titles.

That was, until now.

For the first time, Georgiana wished she was the daughter of a peer, like her mother, so she would be allowed to flirt with the Duke of Rothford and encourage his affections.

His Grace escorted the Darcys to his box, a private balcony that gave them a perfect view of the stage as well as the rest of the theatre. In turn, it would also give everyone else a good view of them. Georgiana wasn't sure what she thought about that. She knew they were still on display and had to prove they were above any accusations of scandal to stamp out any further gossip.

Settling into her cushioned chair, she adjusted her shawl around her shoulders as Elizabeth sat on her left with Fitzwilliam next to her. The Duke sat at on

Georgiana's right.

The ushers snuffed out the lamps, and all at once the theatre quieted as everyone settled into their seats. The play was about to begin.

Georgiana looked over the audience, seeing precious gems twinkle in the dim light. The scent of mingling perfumes was almost overwhelming. From the corner of her eye she saw Lydia in the general seating below, looking up at them. She didn't dare acknowledge her after her mortifying display outside.

"Pay her no mind," the Duke whispered.

"Who?" Georgiana feigned ignorance, hoping he would believe she didn't know who he was referring to.

He nodded towards Lydia. "She is the bitter wife of a military man and wholly unworthy of your concern. You will have better than that one day. I promise."

Georgiana could not reply.

For the first few minutes of the play, Georgiana couldn't think of anything but the words the Duke had spoken: *the bitter wife of a military man*. She realised that would have been her fate had she eloped with Mr. Wickham five years ago.

When she was finally able to turn her attention to the actors, she was delighted by their performance. By the end of the first act she was leaning forward in her seat to better see the stage. When the curtain closed and the lamps were relit for the intermission, Georgiana leaned back in her seat with bright eyes. How she loved the theatre! Turning towards the Duke, she found him watching her. The shimmer of the candlelight reflected in his dark eyes. Her discomfort under his scrutiny made her fidget in her seat.

"What an excellent performance, do you not think so?" he said.

"Indeed, I do." Georgiana had the feeling he wasn't speaking just about the actors, but she couldn't be sure.

"Shall we walk out to the reception area and get something to drink?"

"I would like that." She turned to Elizabeth and her brother. "Would you like to accompany us?"

"You go ahead, we will be along shortly," Elizabeth answered, sitting forward in her chair to look at the crowd below. Georgiana suspected she was searching for Lydia.

Taking the Duke's arm, Georgiana allowed him to guide her out of his box and down the corridor. Many people stopped to speak with the Duke and even more nodded as they passed, but few acknowledged her. When they finally made their way to the refreshment table the Duke handed her a glass of lemonade. A group of well-dressed men recognized the Duke and called him over. Georgiana stood a ways behind him as he shook hands, slapped backs, and struck up a genial conversation.

She wasn't prepared when she heard the horrible velvety voice of Lady Sophia Beck close behind her.

"Do not tell me you are here with the Duke of Rothford," she said flatly.

"What?" Georgiana gasped, turning to face the lady who wasn't very ladylike at all.

"You heard what I said."

"Very well, I will not tell you."

"I'm not asking, not really. I am surprised he's stooped so low as to be seen in your company so many times in one week."

"Why would you say such a thing?" Georgiana asked, shocked by the woman's vicious attacks, in public no less.

"Oh, did I hurt your feelings?" She schooled her expression into a mockery of concern, which quickly changed to a smile as she offered the Duke a friendly nod over Georgiana's shoulder.

Lady Sophia's words were cutting, but Georgiana was determined not to let the woman get the better of her. "I have been through much of late," she said. "There is very little you can say that will shock or hurt me."

Lady Sophia gave a little "hmph!" of disappointment and then suddenly changed tack. "I'm surprised His Grace escorted you here and then left you all alone. Look at him, talking with his friends rather than attending to you." She tossed a sly look at the group of gentlemen. "If he was not ashamed to be seen with you he would have you at his side right now, introducing you to all of his friends."

"His Grace has been a most attentive companion. I have no complaints regarding his treatment of me."

Lady Sophia carried on as if she had not heard. "Honestly, I was surprised he brought you to the theatre with him at all, but then I remembered that he has been trying to hide from my father for weeks now. He knows my father would never deign to suffer your presence, so His Grace is using you as a shield to keep my father away. He thinks he can avoid paying his gambling debts, but it will not work forever." Georgiana's gasp seemed to encourage Lady Sophia. "I cannot blame him, though." She tied the ribbon of her reticule around her wrist. "If I had a similar chance to save my family's reputation and an estate, I can't say I wouldn't stoop so low as to associate with a mere gentleman's daughter, even someone with such low connections as yours. They say your sister-in-law's family is in trade. How droll!"

Georgiana wished she were anywhere but in Lady Sophia's presence. She couldn't say a word, for if she did she was sure to cry, and she refused to give Lady Sophia the satisfaction.

Another false smile flashed across Lady Sophia's face as Georgiana felt a gentle hand at her elbow. "Lady Sophia." The Duke of Rothford's voice sounded hard. "How good it is to see you this evening. I'm sorry to interrupt, but I am afraid I must claim Miss Darcy. I wish to introduce her to some friends of mine."

"Of course. I hope we have the pleasure of seeing each other again." Lady Sophia curtsied and simpered with the most affected sincerity Georgiana had ever witnessed.

Georgiana returned the curtsey and then allowed the Duke to present her to his friends. She met so many people she was sure she would never remember all their names. It was a great relief when the Duke suggested they return to his box for the second act.

When they took their seats Elizabeth and Fitzwilliam had not yet returned to the box, so they had a few minutes of private conversation. The Duke wasted no time in addressing the cause of Georgiana's discomfiture, proving he was far more observant and attentive than Lady Sophia would have her believe.

"Miss Darcy, although I couldn't hear what was said, I watched your conversation with Lady Sophia. I am sorry if she distressed you. Please, do not credit a word she says."

"I will try, but what she said was very upsetting and it will be hard for me to simply set it aside."

"Do not let her affect you. She is a spiteful soul."

"And you are the target of her spite?"

The Duke tugged at his cravat, taking longer to respond than Georgiana would have expected. At last he said, "This is not the time or place to discuss it. Some other time, perhaps."

Georgiana couldn't help but notice that the good mood he had displayed earlier was gone. His thoughts appeared to be every bit as dark as her own.

Chapter Ten

Fitzwilliam and Elizabeth returned to their seats. If either one noticed the altered mood in the box, neither made mention of it. When the candles were once again extinguished, Georgiana released a breath she had not realized she'd been holding. It was far too hard to hide her emotions from the Duke and her family when the candles illuminated the theatre and its patrons in a romantic glow. She hardly paid any attention to the second act, and the longer it dragged on the more distressed she became.

When the second act finally ended, Georgiana refused the Duke's offer to walk the corridor and instead asked him to bring her another glass of lemonade. He understood her reluctance and left her in the box with Mrs. Darcy while he and Mr. Darcy went to fetch refreshments. Once they were out of sight, Elizabeth turned to Georgiana. "I hope you weren't affected by what Lydia said when we arrived this evening."

Georgiana shook her head and massaged her temples. "It wasn't Lydia who distressed me."

"Then who? Was it His Grace? Has he done or said something to hurt you?" When Georgiana didn't respond right away, Elizabeth's concern deepened. "Oh, Georgie! What did he do? What did he say?"

"It was not him directly. When we were getting refreshments after the first act he left me for a moment to speak with some friends and Lady Sophia accosted me again. It was she who distressed me."

"Good Lord, what is the matter with her?" Elizabeth huffed in exasperation. "Would you like to go home? I am sure His Grace would understand."

"No. I do not wish to inconvenience His Grace. He is enjoying the play and is already aware of Lady Sophia speaking with me. He has asked me not to believe her and offered to speak with me about it later."

"All right, but if you change your mind you need only say the word and I will have your brother ask the Duke to take us home directly."

Georgiana had just finished thanking Elizabeth when the gentlemen returned. She felt better after sharing her distress with her sister-in-law. Her brother and the Duke entered the box in the middle of a conversation about their hunting dogs. Each had their favourite breed and neither would allow the other their due merit in the debate. Their playful discussion did a lot to ease her nerves.

Soon the candles were extinguished for the third act. As the last one was snuffed, she caught sight of

Lady Sophia watching them from another box across the theatre. The malice in her gaze seemed to magnify in the darkness. Georgiana shivered.

The Duke noticed her tremor and adjusted her shawl for her, lightly brushing his fingers across her arm in the process. The sensation produced by the barest touch of his fingertips on her skin surprised her. She turned towards him just a little and gave him a small smile.

"That is better," he whispered in her ear before returning his attention to the play. She saw his smile and knew he was pleased. She wasn't certain of her own feelings. It had taken all of her strength to smile even that little bit. Her instinct had been to move her arm away, but she hadn't done it because another part of her wanted so much more than just the light brush of his fingertips across her upper arm. She was sure he must be unaware of the effect he had on her.

When the actors took their final curtain call, Georgiana had never been so relieved for a play to be over. She could scarcely remember what she had seen for all her inner turmoil regarding Lydia's outburst, Lady Sophia's venomous words, and then the Duke's light touch. She hoped she answered coherently when the Duke asked her thoughts about a certain scene, but she couldn't be sure. Her thoughts were too jumbled.

When they stepped into the corridor it was already full of theatre patrons moving towards the exit. Georgiana followed Elizabeth, who was being led by her brother through the throng in front of her. She could feel the Duke's hand on the small of her back, protecting her from the rushing mob threatening to press against her. Darting her eyes back and forth over the crowd, she kept a constant lookout for both of the women she hoped to avoid.

"Who are you looking for?" the Duke asked, interrupting her thoughts.

"No one."

"Are you sure? You look as if you are looking for someone in particular."

"I am not so much looking for someone as hoping to avoid them," Georgiana admitted.

"Mrs. Wickham?"

"She is one."

"And Lady Sophia?"

"Yes, she is the other."

"You have nothing to fear, I will not allow her near you again. I promise."

"How can you make such a promise, Your Grace? It is not as if you can always be at my side to deter her."

Her boldness seemed to surprise him. "I suppose I will just have to visit you more often so she has fewer opportunities to find you alone."

The Duke almost bowled over Georgiana when she stopped short in front of him and turned to stare at him in shock.

"Do you object to my visits, Miss Darcy?"

Georgiana turned away and quickened her step in pursuit of her brother and his wife. "Of course not,

Your Grace. I am just a little surprised you plan to continue them."

"Why should I not? I have had nothing but amiable experiences calling upon you and your family."

Georgiana glanced around her and noticed more than one woman glaring at her as she walked with the Duke. "Look around you, Your Grace."

The Duke took a moment to scan the vicinity. "Ah yes, I see. It is uncommon for a duke to call upon a lady whose father is not titled."

"I believe your invitations to me and my family are causing quite a stir around London."

"I have no doubt they are, but I care not what London society thinks. It is not as if they have dealt the two of us a pretty hand as of late."

"That much is true." Georgiana spoke hesitantly, torn between wanting to encourage him and knowing he would surely break her heart if she did.

"If you will allow me, I will brave society's disapproval and call on you tomorrow afternoon. I believe the two of us must speak about a certain disagreeable lady of our acquaintance."

"I look forward to it, Your Grace."

Chapter Eleven

The morning was well advanced by the time Georgiana awoke. She had lain awake far into the night replaying her conversations with Lady Sophia and the Duke, and now she was afraid she had slept right through breakfast. She dressed hastily in a yellow morning dress and twisted her hair up in a sloppy bun without her maid's help, then rushed downstairs.

The breakfast room was empty when she entered. She rang the bell and the housekeeper answered her summons. "I'm sorry, Miss Darcy, breakfast has been cleared away an hour at least. Would you like me to get you a tray?"

"Yes, thank you. Do you know where Mrs. Darcy is?"

"She is in the library with Mr. Darcy and Colonel Fitzwilliam."

"Then I shall join them. Have the tray brought to the library." She turned to go and then paused with her hand on the door jamb. "Oh, and add a little extra, please. You know how my cousin is."

Georgiana experienced a moment of dread as she approached the library, wondering if perhaps Richard had come to bring news of yet another vicious rumour. She shook her head and tried to banish the thought. It would be a hard thing indeed if her experiences this season taught her to fear her beloved cousin's coming. Taking a deep breath and dredging up a smile from somewhere, she opened the library door.

"Sweetling, it is good to see you looking so well," Richard said warmly, rising from his seat and offering her a kiss on the cheek. "Pray tell me, are you enjoying your regained freedom?"

"Yes I am, in spite of everything. Has Elizabeth told you all that happened at the theatre last night?"

"I have," Elizabeth confirmed.

"I must confess, I was shocked by what she said. Lady Sophia truly approached you a second time about the Duke's personal affairs, and while you were in his company?" Richard looked between Georgiana, Elizabeth, and Fitzwilliam.

"Yes, she did," Georgiana answered, reluctantly recalling the scene once more. "She also made it very clear she expects people to associate only with those of their same social standing. She finds it very offensive that the Duke of Rothford has asked us to accompany him to Almack's and Drury Lane."

"I can well believe that. Members of the peerage expect a duke shall marry no one save she be a duke's daughter, and marquesses, earls, viscounts, and barons all believe exactly the same. How else would the men retain their long necks and slender figures if it didn't continually run in the family?"

"Richard, you are horrible."

Georgiana was still scolding him for his unflattering speech when her breakfast tray arrived along with the tea service. Richard stayed long enough to devour a second breakfast before he left. The entirety of their conversation for once did not revolve around Georgiana and scandals, which she was thankful for. She was tired of being the centre of every discussion. Richard had made much progress on the case of Captain Wickham's being in town. He thought it very likely the man had run out of leave and may be arrested on charges of desertion. Georgiana couldn't understand why he hadn't been arrested already, but apparently he had gone into hiding.

After seeing Richard out, Georgiana went to the sitting room window and watched him leave. He waved up at her. She returned the gesture and then retreated to the music room, seeking comfort in her music.

Georgiana wasn't expecting the Duke of Rothford until late afternoon, so when she looked up from her piano and saw him standing in the doorway of the music room she thought he was a figment of her imagination.

"Miss Darcy," he said with a polite bow, "your playing is beautiful."

She slid off the bench and stood to curtsey,

mortified that he had caught her still in her plain morning dress. "Your Grace, I did not expect you so early." A hand flew to her hair as she realised the mess she must look with her hasty bun hanging at the nape of her neck. Loose strands floated about her head in a halo.

"It is after two o'clock," the Duke replied, looking slightly uncomfortable. "I apologise for coming in unannounced. Mrs. Darcy is having tea brought to the sitting room and I impulsively offered to fetch you myself. Would you prefer I return later?"

Tucking a loose strand of hair behind her ear, she said, "That won't be necessary, Your Grace. Only … please excuse my appearance."

"You need not worry about your appearance," the Duke said as he walked with her to the sitting room. "I think you look lovely."

"Your eyesight must be failing you. I slept quite late and dressed without the help of my maid. I know perfectly well how dreadful I look. Tease me if you must. I deserve to be mocked for my sloth." Georgiana wanted him to see her as a strong woman, not one easily intimidated, though indeed she wasn't nearly as confident as she sounded.

"I do not tease. I will say it again: I think you look lovely."

Georgiana looked away shyly, losing all pretence of confidence. Elizabeth took one look at them when they entered the sitting room together and accurately gauged the situation. She took her tea and her embroidery basket to a chair by the window and tried to be unobtrusive while maintaining a watchful eye on her charge.

"Your sister is the perfect chaperone," the Duke remarked as he took a seat and accepted a cup of tea from a very flustered Georgiana. "She maintains all sense of propriety whilst allowing us private conversation."

"Yes, but I assure you her senses are attuned to everything. She misses nothing."

"Nothing?" the Duke questioned.

Georgiana sat across from the Duke, casting a glance at her sister-in-law in time to see her lips turn up in an amused smile. "Absolutely nothing."

"And last night? Did she miss nothing then?"

"I think it is safe to assume so." Georgiana blushed a becoming shade of red.

"Yet she said nothing at the time."

"Perhaps she is relying on your honour as a gentleman."

He laughed. "Duly noted." He took her hand, raised it to his lips, and kissed the back of it.

Georgiana's pulse quickened. She did not want to pull away, but she heard Elizabeth clear her throat from her seat across the room. Quickly, she withdrew her trembling hand and sat back. "See, what did I tell you? Perhaps we should dispense with the pleasantries and get to the purpose of your visit. I believe we were going to discuss the strange behaviour of Lady Sophia Beck."

"There's certainly no beating around the bush with you, is there?"

"Under the circumstances, I am sure you can agree it is for the best. I understand Mr. Darcy has already informed you of my previous encounter with Lady Sophia."

"He has, and I would very much like to know all that Lady Sophia has said to you. I hope you will then allow me to defend myself."

"That is just what I hope. This will be hard for me, so please bear with me."

The Duke nodded and remained silent while she gathered her thoughts. There were so many rumours about his family; he could only image what she had been told.

When Georgiana was ready, she told him of last night's encounter with Lady Sophia. She left nothing out, relating the entire conversation as exactly as she could. The Duke was quite angry by the end of her recitation; he was fairly quivering with pent-up rage. Perhaps it was a family trait that had given Rothrage Castle its name.

"Is that all she has said?" The Duke ran a hand through his hair, tousling the perfectly combed strands.

"Is that not enough?"

"That is not what I meant. I mean to ask if you are finished."

"Oh, yes, I am."

"First of all, let me apologize for her horrible manners. I am very sorry she has offended you."

"Your Grace, you need not apologize for her. She would not do the same for herself."

"You are right, but I do it all the same. It is unfathomable to me how people can treat others so abominably." He raked his hand through his hair a second time. "I wish I could refute everything she says, but there is a portion of truth in it. I am sure a man in your brother's position has had experience with someone twisting the truth against him for their own gain."

"He has."

"Most men of property have. Allow me to explain. My father had a long history with Lord Mardsen, Lady Sophia Beck's father. I would not say the two were friends, but since our lands abut each other it was impossible to ignore him. I have known Lady Sophia and her family all my life, but like my father and hers, I would not say we are friends either. My elder brother, Geoffrey, felt otherwise. The day before he died, he asked Lord Mardsen for his daughter's hand in marriage. He was accepted by father and daughter, but he died before informing our family of the engagement. The banns were never read and my family knew nothing of it until a few days after my brother's funeral. Lady Sophia and her father came to me at that time and told me of her understanding with my brother. Lord Mardsen informed me that he expected me to honour the engagement in my brother's stead. I refused.

"You see, Lady Sophia desired nothing more than to be the Duchess of Rothford and to live at Rothrage Castle. I am quite certain she never loved Geoffrey, whatever she may have led him to believe. Needless to say, Lord Mardsen was not satisfied with my response. Unbeknownst to me, he went to my father and requested the same. My father saw merit in the union and entered into an agreement on my behalf. When my father told me of the arrangement I related to him the details of my interview with Lord Mardsen, of which he was unaware. I assured him I would hold fast to my refusal despite the marriage agreement he had entered into. My father was upset at having been duped and resolved to release me from the agreement. He and I went to Lord Mardsen that very day and the agreement was dissolved.

"That was nearly ten years ago, just before my eighteenth birthday. I returned to school, thinking that would be the last of my interactions with Lord Mardsen and his daughter, other than the usual business dealings between two masters whose lands abut one another's. I was very wrong." Lowering his eyes, he slowly shook his head. "Upon my father's death six months ago—God, I will never forget that horrible day—his steward informed me that there was one matter requiring my immediate attention: the transfer of Rothrage Manor to Lord Mardsen. Rothrage Manor is the secondary estate within the Rothford duchy. It is of no small consequence with a sizeable income that my brother, Lord Rickords, is to have. *Was* to have," he corrected himself bitterly.

"Oh no!" Georgiana exclaimed, her hand flying to her mouth.

"The part I have yet to disclose to a single soul beyond my brother and my solicitor is how the estate was lost. My father, who was not in his right mind as he neared death, was caught up in a wager with the Marquess. You see, my father loved breeding Thoroughbreds for the races, though he was a terrible judge of horse flesh. Not many months before Father passed, Lord Mardsen had occasion to see the horse he was, in his delusion, hoping to enter at Ascot. Lord Mardsen, a considerably better judge of horse flesh, knew an inbred, weak-legged creature when he saw one. He scoffed at the poor beast's chances, which enraged my father. He challenged Lord Mardsen to a race: his Thoroughbred against the best the Mardsen stables had to offer. So confident was he in success that he was persuaded to wager Rothrage Manor on the outcome. He lost, of course, and was too ashamed to tell me and my brother."

"I am so sorry," Georgiana said when he paused in his story.

"I have been working with a team of solicitors to keep the estate in our family. We've had it almost a hundred years; I refuse to let it go without a fight."

"Will Lord Mardsen not accept monetary payment in lieu of the estate? Surely he understands your father's mind may not have been whole and will not force you to relinquish it."

"Unfortunately, Miss Darcy, there are men in this world who do not always do the honourable thing. I believe the Marquess intentionally goaded my father into making the wager. The estate is far more valuable as a source of continual income, and since he has witnesses who can swear to my father promising it to him, our own honest stable master among them, he is in the right to demand it as payment. As I said, I have men working to keep it, but at this time I am unsure of what the outcome may be."

"Have you any chance of prevailing?" Georgiana asked hopefully.

The Duke rubbed his hands together and woefully replied, "It is not looking promising."

"I wish you all the luck in the world. I can only imagine the anguish this must be causing you."

"I hope you will exonerate me of Lady Sophia's vicious accusations. She has never forgiven me for slighting her. It is her intent to hurt everyone with whom I associate."

"Of course, I understand. You and your father are not the only ones who have been the victim of persons with evil intent."

"I am sorry she has hurt you too."

"She has hurt me, it is true, but I was thinking of someone else who did me a far worse injury."

"Who could possibly wish to hurt you, Miss Darcy? You are goodness personified."

Georgiana blushed again, distressed at how easily this man could discompose her. "I don't believe this person's intent was to hurt me directly, but rather to strike at my brother through me. I was only a means to an end. It pains me to speak of it, but as it may have some bearing on our present difficulties, I believe I must. Perhaps knowing the whole history will help you make sense of all that has happened this last fortnight. Mr. Darcy told you of Captain George

Wickham, did he not?"

"He did. He was the person you saw in Regent's Park speaking with Lady Sophia. I had never heard of the man before and cannot think what connection to the Marquess's children he might have. I am sorry to cause you more pain, but if what you have to say can elucidate matters, pray continue."

"Did my brother tell you anything of our family's history with Captain Wickham?"

"He gave me to understand your family has known him for many years and he is not to be trusted."

"No, indeed." Georgiana took a deep breath and straightened her skirts. "George Wickham was the son of my father's steward at Pemberley. He was a friend and playmate to my brother in their youth, and I myself once looked upon him as a sort of elder foster brother. My father thought highly of him and even went so far as to provide for him in his will, leaving to him a valuable family living. Mr. Wickham, as he was then, refused the living and received in its stead a large sum of money. How he fell into his profligate ways I know not, but fall he did. When the money was all spent, he went to my brother and requested the living be given to him. My brother refused, of course, and Mr. Wickham turned vengeful eyes on me and my dowry of thirty thousand pounds."

She paused as her eyes filled with tears, recalling the shame of past humiliations. Elizabeth moved as if she would come to her, but Georgiana rallied, cleared her throat, straightened her spine, and continued. Elizabeth settled back in her chair, proud of the strength her sister-in-law was displaying.

"I went to Ramsgate with my companion, who we later discovered was a cohort of Mr. Wickham's. She communicated to him our whereabouts, and he joined us there. You may guess what followed. I believed myself in love, and I am ashamed to say I consented to an elopement. If my brother had not come to visit unannounced … You must understand I was only fifteen. I knew nothing of the world or of Mr. Wickham's altered character. I knew only the kind man whom I thought of as family. To this day the man haunts me."

"Why do you say that?"

"For a multitude of reasons. First, I've lived in constant fear he would tell someone of our almost-elopement. Second, he is Mrs. Darcy's brother-in-law, a marriage brought about by my brother to keep Mr. Wickham from ruining Lydia as he might have ruined me. He is now connected with my family in the most intimate manner."

"You may never be rid of him, but you need never fear him again. You are blameless. The rake tried to take advantage of you when you were still a child. I am glad your brother arrived in time to save you, for there is a far better man out there waiting for you."

Georgiana looked down. She dearly wished he was that man, no matter how impossible she knew it to be.

"Your Grace, were you able to discover why Captain Wickham and Lady Sophia were together?"

"I have not. It is possible he has struck up a

friendship with Lieutenant Beck, the Marquess's younger son. He matches the description of the man you saw with them. I was inclined to believe their association an innocent one, but now that I know the man's true character I shall endeavour to discover more."

"I hope you are able to save Rothrage Manor. I would hate it if Lord Mardsen and his awful daughter prevailed over you."

"Thank you."

The pair sat in silence for almost a minute while they contemplated all they had learned of each other. At last, Georgiana said, "After such a deep conversation, I wonder if you will allow me to play for you. Music always lightens my spirits."

"I would like that very much. I shall turn the pages for you."

Elizabeth stood to follow the pair as the Duke offered Georgiana his arm. He escorted her back to the music room and seated her at the piano bench. Before she could release his arm, he covered her hand with his own and gently caressed the back of it without Elizabeth seeing.

Georgiana released his arm, disappointed to lose his touch, though she was cognizant of the impropriety. She selected a romantic Italian ballad and placed the sheets in front of her. She had the music memorised, which was fortunate since the Duke spent more time looking at her than attending to his page-turning duties. Twice she had to prompt him, but she did not mind.

Walking him to the door at the end of his visit, Georgiana thanked him for coming and told him she looked forward to seeing him again soon. She waited in the open door while he mounted his white horse and rode away, saluting her like a knight of old.

Chapter Twelve

Slowly and reluctantly, Georgiana opened her eyes. Streaks of sunlight penetrated the sheer window coverings, the sort of weak winter light that brought no warmth. She had asked Mary to leave the heavy drapes open last night so she could stargaze while she brushed her hair. The sky had proved too overcast for stargazing, and she had forgotten to close the drapes before she went to bed.

She sat up and rubbed her knuckles into her dreamy eyes. Mary was ready for her with heated wash water and curling tongs. Today was the Sabbath and the family planned to attend the early church services.

Dressed in a simple but pretty gown, Georgiana picked up her prayer book and met her brother and Elizabeth in the breakfast room.

"Good morning," she said in a tone much more energetic than she felt.

"You are up early this morning," Darcy said, spreading his toast with preserves.

"It's not that early." Georgiana laid her prayer book on the table then went to the sideboard to prepare a plate.

"It is early compared to the hours you've kept lately."

"One can hardly judge based on that." Taking her seat, she picked up her napkin and shook it out. "I plan to put the last fortnight behind me."

"I think that is an excellent idea. I see you brought your prayer book down. I am glad. I wasn't sure if you would want to attend church with us today."

"Why wouldn't I?" Georgiana asked. "My presentation to the patronesses at Almack's was a great success and we have at last overcome the awful lies that were bandied about London."

"The rumours have not entirely gone away," her brother corrected her, "but I agree they have been sufficiently suppressed so as to not cause any lasting damage."

Georgiana couldn't help searching for the Duke of Rothford as she sat in the pew next to her brother. She had never seen him at their parish before and did not expect to see him today, but she could hope. Her mind thus occupied, she hardly remembered a word of the service when it was over.

The Darcys had never experienced a great crush of people vying for their attention after church. In the past they had always been able to leave unmolested after thanking the clergyman and speaking to three or four neighbours. That was not the case today. News of Georgiana being escorted around London by the Duke of Rothford had spread far and wide. It seemed the whole parish wanted to hear Miss Darcy's first-hand account of everything His Grace had said or done. Some whispered their envy behind concealing fans; some criticised the Darcys for encouraging Georgiana's apparent and shocking ambition. The attention was staggering to someone like Georgiana, who preferred to blend into the crowd and remain forgotten.

Mr. and Mrs. Darcy were both pulled aside at some point by eager gossips. Upon finding herself alone in what seemed to her a voracious mob, Georgiana began to panic. When she spotted her brother at bottom of the church stairs, she gave silent thanks and made to move towards him, hoping Elizabeth was with him so they might take their leave immediately.

"Miss Darcy! Oh, Miss Darcy!" Icy prickles danced up Georgiana's spine when she heard the venomous voice of Lady Sophia Beck. "Fancy seeing you here. I'll wager we have attended the same services fifty times together and did not even realise it. Too bad the Duke of Rothford is not here. Then again, he rarely attends church. His character is ill-suited for spiritual pursuits."

Georgiana didn't reply. She no longer felt obligated to avoid slighting the woman now that she knew the whole of the history between her family and the Duke.

"I did hear His Grace has called upon you more

than once. Is it true?"

"It is." Georgiana refused to expand upon her answer.

"I'm sorry you will no longer be able to enjoy his company as you have been; I am sure his notice must have been quite incomparable. Now that he is gone out of the city, you must surely feel his loss. Oh, I see! He did not tell you he was leaving, did he? What a blow that must be! I did hear, however, that your imposition on his notice has garnered you the attention of other gentlemen that heretofore had no notion of you in your past seasons. Perhaps you will not miss him at all since you were only using him to gain acceptance by those of higher rank."

Georgiana was struck speechless by these wild accusations. She saw Elizabeth weaving through the crowd to Fitzwilliam's side and tried to catch her attention. It was to no avail; she did not look up.

Lady Sophia saw the object of her gaze and smiled coldly. "Your sister-in-law can have no time for you, I am sure. She must worry about her own position. She may have been a gentleman's daughter when she married your brother, but her connections are of the lowest sort in London. She cannot afford to have you jeopardise her social standing because you have the presumption to aspire to an impossible match. You should know the Duke of Rothford will never marry you; I am determined he shall marry *me*." Georgiana could not hide her shock that Lady Sophia would say such a thing, aloud, and in a public place, no less. "My father is going to arrange it all. I have it on good authority the Duke wants nothing more in this world than to preserve Rothrage Manor for his wretched younger brother, so I am sure it will soon be accomplished." Her smile became more a sneer than anything else. "Well, I have much to do. I look forward to our next meeting, Miss Darcy."

Lady Sophia pranced away, throwing frequent glances back at Georgiana, which disconcerted her. Georgiana stood frozen in place for a long time, clasping her shaking hands inside her muff, until Elizabeth collected her and led her to the Darcy carriage with a reassuring grip on her elbow. It wasn't until the carriage moved away from the church that her hands finally steadied in her lap.

Georgiana was glad that Elizabeth and Fitzwilliam were too busy talking to each other to notice she was out of sorts.

A home, Georgiana rushed to her rooms and collapsed on her bed in tears. It had taken all of her strength not to cry in the carriage, but now in the privacy of her rooms she was free to give vent to her feelings. It was some time before she felt equal to joining her brother and his wife in the library. When she entered, Fitzwilliam and Elizabeth were sitting together in front of the fire, engrossed in their books. Elizabeth was snuggled in the crook of his arm. She looked happy. Content.

Georgiana selected a book at random and took a seat opposite them.

Elizabeth watched her for some time before breaking the silence. "Georgiana, is something the matter?"

"No, not a thing." Georgiana played with the pages of her book, a sure tell that something was in fact bothering her.

Elizabeth worried about Georgiana; her emotions since their difficulties had begun were far more erratic than they had ever been in the four years she had known her. This morning she had been happy and now, half a day later, she was working herself into a frenzy, over what, she knew not.

Fitzwilliam understood, like his wife did, that something was wrong. He had found that when these situations arose it was best for him to retreat and allow Elizabeth to work her magic with his sister. Elizabeth understood Georgiana in ways he never would. He trusted her to calm his sister's troubled spirit. Dismissing himself, Fitzwilliam departed the library, leaving the ladies to talk.

"Dearest, you are going to ruin that book if you keep mauling the pages like that."

Georgiana hastily closed the book and left her seat to put it back on the shelf where it belonged. "I am fine, I promise."

"I do not believe you." A teasing sparkle ignited in Elizabeth's eyes. "Did His Grace ride a different horse yesterday? It would be a depressing thing indeed had he ridden a black one."

"Even if he had I would not give you the satisfaction of knowing something so silly affected me." Georgiana returned to her seat and looked into the fire. "I wish it were that simple."

"If it is not his horse, then what is bothering you? I will not believe there is nothing."

"Did you interrogate your own sisters so before you came to us?"

"Yes, and they never succeeded at resisting, so you may as well give in and tell me now."

Georgiana gave her a rueful smile and relented. "After church I was stopped by Lady Sophia Beck."

"Again? She has a nasty habit of cornering you when you least expect it."

"You are correct. She also has a habit of distressing me."

"What did she say this time?"

"Nothing of consequence."

"If that was the case then you wouldn't be so out of sorts."

Georgiana sighed and told her about Lady Sophia's insults regarding the Darcys' social position. "I am sure it is nothing. I am just being silly."

Elizabeth did not at first respond, but then her face clouded and she said, "Georgie, have you developed tender feelings for the Duke?" When Georgiana did not answer, she said, "Dearest, I warned you against allowing your feelings to become engaged."

"Elizabeth, it is not as if I can help it."

"You must try. I have already explained to you that the Duke has extended invitations and repeatedly called on you because he is a kind man. He only seeks to ensure that the vicious rumours which circulated around London have no lasting effect on you. His feelings are not likely to be engaged, and you must give up all expectations and hopes of such."

"Elizabeth, I know that I may never engage the Duke's affections as he has mine, but what harm is there in a little wishful thinking?"

"If it was only wishful thinking I would not be so concerned, but this is more than that. You are letting your heart be affected."

"Be at ease; it will pass soon enough. I have been informed His Grace has left London for a time, and so my life shall go on, and he shall not be part of it."

"I see what is happening. Correct me if I am wrong, but I suspect Lady Sophia Beck not only criticized your social position, but also was the one to inform you of His Grace's departure from town." Georgiana nodded. "Would it have been better or worse if he had told you himself?"

A tear slipped down Georgiana's cheek.

"Georgie, I do not want to upset you, but these are things you must think about. I am sure His Grace had no notion he had engaged your feelings for the simple reason that he wasn't trying."

"That is enough, Elizabeth. I understand you."

Elizabeth watched Georgiana closely. "You may not believe it, but I know what you are feeling. There was a time, once I had come to love your brother, when I was sure we could never be together. I regretted the day we had been introduced to one another because I associated it with the beginning of my misery."

"But, Elizabeth, you must have had hope at some

point. Look at you now. You and
been married for more than four yea
is true, and I suspect it is, my feeli
reciprocated. At least you and Fitzw
same sphere, which made your mar
The Duke is so far above our station that I have no
hope at all."

"And that, dearest, is the harm in wishful thinking."

Georgiana had had enough and resolved to seek
solitude elsewhere. She took her leave and then
paused at the door, saying, "Do not worry, Elizabeth,
I shall get over this."

Chapter Thirteen

Two days passed with no word of the Duke of Rothford. Retiring to her room early on Tuesday, Georgiana was downcast. She had taken to pacing her room and, when at last she lay upon her bed, she had trouble sleeping as her head ached acutely.

On Wednesday when the grey morning light filtered into her room, Georgiana sat up in bed, disoriented. It felt as if she had just fallen asleep. The dishevelled bedclothes wrapped around her attested to her broken sleep.

The headache, which had started last night, was now the beginning of a migraine. With a groan, she lay back against her pillows and closed her eyes.

She was still abed when a downstairs maid came in to stoke the fire. Removing the fire screen, she took the poker and stirred the embers before placing another log on the fire. They crackled, sending sparks flying up the chimney. When she noticed Georgiana was awake, she enquired, "Are you ill, Miss Darcy?"

"It is only a little headache."

"Would you like a tray brought up?"

"Yes, that would be nice." Georgiana pushed herself up and leaned against the headboard. "And please ask Mrs. Darcy to attend me at her convenience."

"Of course," the girl said, coming to Georgiana's side to straighten the bed covers and fluff the pillows behind her back.

Georgiana smoothed the bed covers over her lap, leaning her head back and closing her eyes until she heard a light knock at her door. Before she could react, the door opened and Elizabeth quietly slipped in and came to her bedside. The maid entered behind her and, at Elizabeth's instruction, left the breakfast tray at the foot of the bed.

"I am told you are not feeling well," Elizabeth said softly.

"My head aches most dreadfully."

"I think a little rest is all you need. You have not slept since learning the Duke of Rothford has left town." Georgiana studied her hands, unable to look Elizabeth in the eyes. "I am right, am I not?"

"Yes, I suppose you are."

"How can I help?"

"I am not sure you can."

"There must be something we can do. Georgiana, you cannot let this affect you so."

"I cannot help it."

"I know it is difficult, but, dearest, you are making yourself ill. I cannot allow that. I am sure His Grace would not approve either, if he knew." When

Georgiana did not reply, Elizabeth understood.

Elizabeth poured Georgiana a cup of tea and handed it to her. "Once you eat you will feel much better. Then I will help you dress. I am sure all you need is a little activity to distract your mind from these gloomy thoughts." She set the breakfast tray on Georgiana's lap. "I just received word that Jane and Charles are in town for a few weeks. Would you like to join me when I call on them?"

Nibbling on the corner of her toast, Georgiana thought for a moment. "I don't wish to give offense, but I do not feel equal to meeting with anyone today."

"Do you really mean that? Dearest, this is Jane we are speaking of. When has she ever failed to make either of us smile?"

"What if I don't want to smile?"

"Very well, I shall not make you visit. I will even allow you to remain in bed and wallow in your own self-pity, but you only get one day. Tomorrow you must rise, get dressed, and greet the day like the old friend it has always been."

"Thank you, Elizabeth, I promise I shall be down tomorrow."

Elizabeth left Georgiana's room a little distressed that she could not persuade her to see Jane. Georgiana was always eager to see Jane. Elizabeth was determined to speak to her sister and hear what she had to say on the subject. Jane was no stranger to grief brought on by the absence of the man she thought she loved in vain. Perhaps she would know how to help Georgiana.

Georgiana remained in bed much of the morning, but found it impossible to sleep. Her mind was far too active, which caused her to be more irritable than she had been the past month combined.

Elizabeth came up after her visit with Jane and told her they would all be attending the opera on Friday. Georgiana momentarily allowed her excitement to rise until she was reminded that she could not accidentally run into the Duke for he was not in town. She longed to see him again, even if only from afar.

At long last, when the sun had sunk below the horizon and night returned, Georgiana slept from pure exhaustion.

Thursday began just as miserably as the days before, but she knew Elizabeth would have her carried bodily from her bed if need be. Georgiana dressed and went downstairs where she paced the sitting room, played a few gloomy sonatas on the piano, and attempted to draw. Deeming her efforts dreadful, she tore up the page and threw the pieces into the fire.

For the rest of the day she was fidgety and restless. Nothing could occupy her for long, and she retired early in a desperate attempt to escape her relentless thoughts.

She had been five whole days without hearing from or seeing the Duke of Rothford and her mind was concocting a dozen reasons why she would never see him again. She had distressed herself so much that she awoke the following morning with a pillow still wet from last night's tears.

It took her a full ten minutes to gather her resolve to ring the bell for Mary and force herself to get out of bed and get dressed.

She may have woken up in bad humour, but the prospect of going to the opera with Charles and Jane Bingley helped to lift her spirits as the day progressed. She could not deny that she hoped the Duke would be there so she could catch the tiniest glimpse of him. That was all she needed, she was sure of it.

Chapter Fourteen

Georgiana's anticipation was palpable as her party slowly ascended the stairs of the Theatre Royal into the crush of the entrance hall. Georgiana felt Fitzwilliam stiffen against the crowd as she walked on his arm. People were chattering and swirling in complete disorder. There was a flurry of silk, velvet, lace, and jewels. Searching the crowd, she looked for a single familiar face and listened for a deep bass voice, but to no avail.

Fitzwilliam and Elizabeth talked amiably with Charles and Jane, but Georgiana's attention constantly roamed the room for any sign of the Duke of Rothford. The closer it came to the overture the heavier her heart became. She felt like running back to the carriage when her brother turned to her and said, "Perhaps we should take our seats. The opera is about to begin."

Her spirits were too low to enjoy the opera and halfway through she begged Fitzwilliam and Elizabeth to take her home. Though they were enjoying their time with Jane and Charles, they understood Georgiana's distress and agreed. While waiting for their carriage to be brought around, Georgiana said, "Thank you for obliging me. I am sorry I spoiled your evening with Charles and Jane."

"Do not worry," Elizabeth said. "We shall have ample opportunities to visit with my sister and Mr. Bingley. But, Georgie, do not think I cannot see what you are doing. You know His Grace is not in London. You cannot expect him to appear at the opera, and yet your pretty head has not stopped swivelling on your neck since we arrived."

"It cannot hurt to hope, can it?"

"If that were true we would not be waiting for our carriage now. We have been through this already. You know nothing can come of this. You are setting yourself up for disappointment. It is not healthy."

Their name was called, effectively cutting off their conversation, much to Georgiana's relief. Fitzwilliam led them out and handed them into the carriage before stepping in and giving the command to take them home.

Three more days passed and Georgiana's mood became more forlorn and depressed. By the following Tuesday, she was refusing leave her rooms again. She didn't eat. She didn't sleep. More often than not she did no more than sit in the window seat with an afghan over her legs and watch travellers pass on the road below. Each time a man rode by on a white horse, her thoughts flew to the Duke. He had seemed so attentive to her, especially during his last visit. She was sure he was enjoying her company, even encouraging her affections despite their different stations in life. What had happened?

On Wednesday morning at a few minutes past eleven, her brother came to speak to her and would brook no refusal.

"Georgiana, I'm afraid I cannot allow you to continue to hide in your room away from the family." Fitzwilliam's words were kind, but said in a stern voice that commanded obedience. "I need you to rise, get dressed, and come downstairs for the remainder of the day. Then, from each day forward, unless you are genuinely ill, I would like you to eat breakfast with Elizabeth and me."

Georgiana did not dare to look him in the eyes.

"I would like it if you would come downstairs within an hour. Do you think you can do that?"

Georgiana nodded.

"Very good. I will leave you to your toilette."

Fifty minutes later, Georgiana appeared in the sitting room where Fitzwilliam and Elizabeth were sitting together. When she entered, they stopped talking and turned their attention to her.

"Good morning," Elizabeth said.

"Good morning," Georgiana answered and then took a seat in the chair across from them.

"Are you hungry? Would you like some tea?"

"No, I thank you. I am not hungry."

The trio sat in silence for a long time, struggling to find the right words to say to each other. At last, Fitzwilliam said, "Georgiana, I am glad you came down. I know how hard it must be for you, but I am confident you will not regret it. Soon you will feel more yourself."

Georgiana nodded, not truly believing her brother's words.

"I thought we could go on a walk in Hyde Park this afternoon. What do you think of the idea?" Elizabeth asked.

"A walk sounds like a fine idea." Georgiana had no desire to go on a walk, but she wasn't sure if her brother would allow her to decline.

"What a fine idea indeed. I shall walk with you, unless you object," Fitzwilliam offered.

"How could we object to such a scheme? I think it would suit us perfectly. Do you not agree, Georgiana?" Elizabeth prompted.

"Yes, brother, you must come." Georgiana's words were everything polite and proper, but they held not the enthusiasm she generally exhibited. It was a start, though, and that was all the Darcys could hope for.

Georgiana tried her best to go about her old daily routine as she thought her brother and Elizabeth expected of her. She spent an hour with her drawing, and another with her music, but her heart wasn't in it.

At four o'clock, the ladies changed into their walking dresses and met Fitzwilliam in the foyer for their walk in Hyde Park. The azure sky overhead sported only a few wispy clouds, which was proving an uncommon occurrence this spring. Mother Nature seemed to have gone mad of late, turning back the seasons and replacing the warmth and renewal of spring with the cold and gloom of winter. For now, the sun shone brightly, golden beams lancing through the boughs of the trees overhead. Georgiana raised her face to catch them, relishing the feel of the warm rays on her skin.

"Good afternoon, Mr. Darcy, Mrs. Darcy, Miss Darcy," the deep rumble of a familiar voice sounded behind them. "I was just on my way to your house when I looked out the carriage window and saw you. I insisted my driver pull over immediately so I could offer my greetings."

Georgiana's heart quickened, drumming in her chest. How she loved his voice, like thunder rolling across the dark skies on a stormy night in the Peak District.

"It is a pleasure to see you, Your Grace." Mr. Darcy bowed.

"Your Grace." Elizabeth curtsied.

Georgiana had trouble responding. After the heaviness she had experienced during her recent depression, the sudden weightlessness she felt surprised her. "Your Grace, we did not expect to see you here," she finally managed to say as she dipped into a curtsey, trying to stop the tingling sensation threatening to race up her arms.

"I can see you did not, but I am glad to have found

you. May I join your outing?"

Georgiana looked to Elizabeth, who nodded her acceptance. "Yes, we would like that."

The Duke offered Georgiana his arm and they set off down the path at an unhurried pace. Fitzwilliam and Elizabeth followed close behind.

Georgiana was far too overcome to speak. Her gaze wandered over everyone and everything except for the one person whom she most wanted to look at. Her eyes were wide and her complexion was glowing when the Duke of Rothford addressed her. "I heard from my brother, Lord Rickords, that you went to the opera last week."

Georgiana looked at him with surprise. "We did, Your Grace. I did not see Lord Rickords there or I would have paid my respects."

"Do not fret; he was not seated near you. He saw you from a distance. He told me you left early. I hope you weren't unwell."

"Thank you, as you can see, we are all quite well."

"I am glad to hear it." He walked in silence for a moment before speaking again. "Have you seen the entire opera in the past, or are you unfamiliar with the ending?"

"Though I have not seen it performed in its entirety, I am familiar with the story."

"Does that mean you would not like to see it again?"

His pace was still unhurried, his outward manner casual, but Georgiana could see he was anxious for her answer. "I should be happy to attend the full opera should I get another chance." Her eyes sparkled and her heart raced as she hoped beyond anything that he would extend the invitation she thought he was hinting at.

"I have not yet attended a performance of this particular opera, and my brother insists I must. Perhaps you and your brother and sister would like to accompany me Saturday night?"

"I would like that, Your Grace. I shall speak with Mr. and Mrs. Darcy and send you word this evening."

"I am also hosting a small dinner party on Friday with some of the friends you met the night we attended the theatre. Would you and Mr. and Mrs. Darcy be my guests? I promise it will be a pleasant diversion. These friends of mine come from all walks of life and our dinners are always lively affairs."

"Again, I shall have to speak with Mr. and Mrs. Darcy, but I hope we will be able to attend. I know of no preferable way to spend Friday and Saturday."

Georgiana noticed his muscles relax as his step became lighter. He seemed more at ease now that his invitations had been extended.

They passed several of his acquaintances on their walk. Each one greeted the Duke and then either offered her a polite nod or ignored her entirely. His Grace kindly returned each greeting but did not stop to speak with any of them. To Georgiana it seemed he was giving her his full attention. How was she to overcome her infatuation with him when he continued to single her out?

For the next twenty minutes, they discussed every

subject acceptable for a single man and woman to address in one another's company. Whenever the Duke took the opportunity to look at Georgiana, he could not help noticing her vivid eyes and parted lips under the brim of her bonnet. She returned his looks, and each saw their own emotions mirrored in the other. The Duke hated to force himself to look away, but he simply could not allow himself to become so fixated on her in public.

"Miss Darcy, I think we must return to the house," Fitzwilliam said, pointedly examining his pocket watch. "Your Grace, you are welcome to walk with us, if you wish."

"Thank you, Mr. Darcy, I shall."

Their conversation returned to more general topics as they all feigned interest in the trees and weather until they reached the edge of the park.

"This is where I must leave you." The Duke released her arm and stepped back. "My carriage is just there." Georgiana turned and saw his glorious carriage with his coat of arms emblazoned on its side waiting for him at the kerb. The liveried footman and driver occupied their proper places with the most dignity she had ever seen in any servants. "As I said, I hope we shall see one another very soon." The Duke bowed and left them.

Georgiana watched him go, waving as the carriage pulled away from the kerb. When she turned her attention to her brother and Elizabeth, she found they were watching her every movement.

A shiver ran up her spine and settled at the nape

of her neck. Her mouth was too moist and she had to swallow before speaking. "Elizabeth, the Duke has invited us to a dinner party at his townhouse on Friday and the Opera on Saturday."

"He has?" Elizabeth was clearly surprised and even a little dismayed.

"Indeed. Do we have plans or may we go? It is the same opera we saw last week. It would be a fine thing to see it to the end, would it not?"

Elizabeth raised an eyebrow at Georgiana. "What do you think, Mr. Darcy?"

"I confess I would very much like to see the entire opera and had thought to suggest it myself."

"What about the dinner party? May we attend it also?" Georgiana was aware of the pleading note in her voice. She was a little ashamed of herself, but she could hardly pretend indifference where the Duke was concerned.

"I know of no other plans," Elizabeth answered with a sigh.

"Then we shall accept both invitations," Fitzwilliam declared.

"Thank you, Fitzwilliam, you are the best brother. And you too, Elizabeth; I could not want for a better sister."

Chapter Fifteen

Georgiana's general mood was one of joyful contentment for the rest of the week. The fact that she had spent days secluded in her room in abject misery was completely forgotten. She laughed easily, smiled almost continually, and more than once was found humming as she went about her day.

Elizabeth and Fitzwilliam could not be happier that her attitude had returned to normal, though they worried twice as much for what lay ahead when the Duke would inevitably withdraw his attentions once again. They were sure the time would soon come.

Georgiana's thoughts were constantly turned to the Duke as she prepared for the dinner party on Friday afternoon. Seeing him in Hyde Park had only confirmed what she had already begun to suspect. She was developing feelings for him, strong feelings, which, she had to admit, were akin to love. Although she could not be sure how he felt, Georgiana was confident he had feelings for her, even if they were slight.

What Georgiana had to determine was whether she could increase the Duke's regard. Could she make him fall in love with her as she was falling in love with him?

Georgiana dressed in an ivory gown for the party. Mary wove red ribbons through her golden curls, their colour making her lips look redder and her cheeks more pink. She was sure to hold the Duke's attention.

When she and Elizabeth had gone shopping at the opening of the season, Georgiana had noticed an ivory shawl made from delicate Brussels lace in a shop window. Normally she didn't buy window fashions because too many other ladies would have the same thing, but she hadn't been able to resist this one. Tonight would be the first time she wore it.

The sun had not yet set when they left for the Duke's townhouse. The carriage skirted the east edge of Hyde Park and then continued south along the west edge of the palace gardens. Rarely had Georgiana been to this part of town, since her brother normally directed the carriage along the northern roads of Piccadilly and Pall Mall.

Georgiana was mesmerized by the Duke's home as her brother handed her down from the carriage. The stark white townhouse was a full five stories tall, six if you counted the attics. Thirty windows and four banisters could be seen on the front alone, and since the building was situated at the end of the block, she was sure if she could peek around the corner she would see as much opulence there as well. A portico with white marble pillars framed the double-door entry. The same marble was used in the balusters on the banisters above.

The door opened before they even had time to knock and they were ushered in by a stately butler and four footmen in the Duke's livery. Their coats and cloaks were efficiently whisked away and the butler led them through the Great Hall, which was lined with five footmen on each side. All ten men were exactly the same height and girth, and the Duke's coat of arms was embroidered upon the jacket cuff of every footman's left arm. The attention to detail was staggering.

When they were announced and shown into the drawing room, Georgiana saw the Duke standing near the fire. He held a glass of wine and talked amiably with his friends. When he saw them he set his glass on the mantle and moved forward to greet them.

Georgiana could hardly breathe as she curtsied to him. "Your Grace, it is good to see you this evening."

The Duke of Rothford could not tear his eyes away from her as he bowed.

Georgiana returned the intensity of his gaze. Her mouth went dry and she licked her lips to moisten them.

Suddenly the Duke straightened and turned to Fitzwilliam and Elizabeth. Georgiana felt him pulling away, but could do nothing.

"Mr. and Mrs. Darcy, Miss Darcy, what a pleasure it is to have you here this evening."

"Your Grace, I brought this for you," Mr. Darcy said, presenting a box to the Duke.

The Duke of Rothford accepted the box and pulled off the lid. Inside was a bottle of the finest Portuguese port to be found in all of London.

"A tawny from Portugal's Douro Valley. A rare bottle indeed," the Duke said with evident pleasure. "This is the Portuguese's favourite; very little of it is exported to England. Thank you, Mr. Darcy."

"You are welcome, Your Grace. I hope you enjoy it."

"I am certain I shall. Come, let me make some introductions."

They followed the Duke across the room and met many of the same friends he had already introduced to Georgiana at the theatre. His "small dinner party" consisted of ten couples. Five of the men Georgiana had already met, and now she met three of their wives as well. They were also introduced to another lady and her chaperone. It was clear she was a woman of status being pursued by one of the single gentlemen in the party.

They took their seats and enjoyed pleasant conversation while they waited for the final three guests to arrive: another single lady and her chaperones. As soon as everyone was present the dinner bell was rung and everyone took their place to go in to the dining room. Georgiana, being so far down in the order of precedence, was unable to go in with the Duke as she would have wished. She and her partner were the lowest ranking and made to go in last. She would have been quite upset had she not arrived in the dining room and found that she and her dinner partner were seated very near the Duke, nearer than she would have ever dreamed possible considering the ranks of those in attendance.

The menu was divine: white soup, roasted veal shanks stuffed with cranberries, dates, sage, and rosemary, wild rice with leeks, roast goose with apples and prunes, stewed pears, Scotch collops, three varieties of fish, oysters in clam sauce, and boiled and braised vegetables of every variety.

All through dinner, Georgiana couldn't keep her eyes off the Duke. Each time she looked at him, every time he spoke, he became more handsome. Twice the Duke addressed her directly. His attention sent shivers of pleasure racing up her spine.

After dinner, the men gathered in the library for drinks while the women waited for them in the drawing room. Georgiana enjoyed getting to know the ladies of the Duke's acquaintance. Soon she was convincing herself she liked them very much and could easily see herself hosting dinner parties for these same women in the future. Although his house was grand and his servants were meticulous, it was not so different from her brother's household that she couldn't see herself managing it. Perhaps some years ago, before Elizabeth had married her brother, Georgiana would have found it daunting, but Elizabeth had taught her so much she was sure she was now equal to the task.

When the men returned from the library, the gathering in the drawing room became a noisy affair with conversations going on in every part of the room. The Duke paid Georgiana particular attention, choosing to sit by her and including her in every conversation.

Partway through the evening the Duke announced, "I'm in the mood for some music. Could I persuade a few of you ladies to play for us? Lady Climson, perhaps?" The lady agreed amiably. "Excellent! Come, follow me to the music room." The Duke offered Georgiana his arm and they led the group into the adjoining room. "Miss Darcy," the Duke spoke low and only for her hearing, "I hope you will also play for us this evening. Rarely have I heard anyone play as well as you."

"Thank you, Your Grace, it would be my pleasure."

Georgiana glanced through the music while Lady Climson and then Lady Sara played, and found one of her favourite pieces in the Duke's collection. When it was her turn she opened the sheet music, settled her slender fingers on the ivory keys, and began to play the Italian opera.

The sweet music soared through the room like spring blossoms on the wind, taking with it the very hearts of everyone listening. But then the music took a turn and the dark and sensual notes stole the breath from their bodies. When the piece was over Georgiana graciously accepted the entire party's effusive praise.

Four more ladies played, including Elizabeth, and then the party returned to the drawing room and began to disperse.

It was late when the Darcys stood to take their leave. Georgiana hated to go but knew they must. Elizabeth looked very tired, and Georgiana didn't want to overstay their welcome and give the Duke any reason to not invite them in the future.

He walked them to the door and held Georgiana's bonnet and gloves while a footman helped her on with her cloak. "Until tomorrow," the Duke said, bowing.

The Darcys stepped out the door into the dark, cold night. As she took her seat in the carriage, Georgiana looked back and saw His Grace leaning against his doorframe, watching them depart. He certainly was a handsome man.

Chapter Sixteen

On Saturday, Georgiana was a bundle of nervous excitement as Mary dressed her hair with pink miniature roses to match her pink gown. The gown had been made just this season and she had not worn it yet.

The feeling of breathlessness came and went in opposition to her tingling hands and the heat that radiated through her chest. All of her senses were heightened: the candles burned brighter, the wine tasted sweeter, and the roses smelled more fragrant.

She was just rising from her vanity when Elizabeth came to fetch her.

"Georgiana, the Duke of Rothford has just arrived. He is downstairs with Fitzwilliam."

"He is ever so punctual, is he not?" Georgiana remarked, gathering her things and handing them to Mary to take downstairs.

"Yes, he is indeed."

Georgiana and Elizabeth walked downstairs and

greeted the gentlemen in the foyer. Georgiana had to resist the impulse to run to the Duke when she saw him. It was soon apparent that she need make no effort to close the distance between them. Her smile rivalled the sun and drew him directly to her side.

"Miss Darcy, it is very good to see you." He bowed low over her hand, though he refrained from kissing it. When he straightened, he retained her hand for rather longer than necessary.

Mr. Darcy cleared his throat loudly and asked, "Shall we go? I know how much Your Grace despises being late for the opening."

"Yes, of course," the Duke said, recollecting himself immediately. "Take care," he admonished, "the steps are a little wet. It seems the fickle heavens have dared to rain on our outing. Here, Miss Darcy, let me help you." Offering her his arm, he led her to the carriage, taking extra care she did not slip on the wet step.

When they arrived at Covent Garden, they rushed through the entrance of the building to make sure the ladies' dresses and slippers were not soiled.

In the cloak room, Georgiana was lightly dabbing at a few raindrops on her face with her delicate handkerchief when the Duke took it and replaced it with his own. "Here, take mine. It will serve you better."

She accepted his handkerchief and used it to pat her face dry. When she tried to give it back to him, he refused to accept it. Her heart skipped a beat when she saw him put hers in his pocket and realised he intended to keep it. She should have demanded he return it, but it made her far too happy to think he would want a keepsake of hers. Quickly, she stowed his out of sight.

Plucking up her courage, she said, "Your Grace, an opera often moves its audience to tears. There may come a time this evening when handkerchiefs will be necessary. Will you be embarrassed to dry your eyes with such a feminine article?"

"I should be more embarrassed to be branded a heartless brute for shedding nary a tear during an aria. But what about you, Miss Darcy? Will that masculine handkerchief disgrace you?"

Georgiana discerned at that moment that Elizabeth was watching her closely. Instead of answering the Duke, she smiled and pressed his hand.

$\mathcal{N}$ever had Georgiana been more disappointed at the conclusion of an opera. The performance was excellent and she had truly enjoyed it this time, but the end came far too quickly for her liking. She could have happily sat in that box beside the Duke for an entire fortnight of operas.

Her euphoria was not to last. They were just leaving their box when Lady Sophia came up behind them. "Your Grace, what a shock it is to see you here this evening." The lady's voice held as much contempt as her looks did when she addressed him. "I had thought you were still in Abingdon."

"Town is vastly more amusing than Abingdon at

present. I returned this week."

"Indeed? I just returned yesterday myself."

"I had not realized you were in Abingdon, Lady Sophia. I hope you had a tolerable journey."

"Surely my father told you I was at Mardsen Manor when the two of you met."

"He did not. We did not discuss personal matters."

"He did not mention it at all? Not once?" Lady Sophia asked, slowly and deliberately moving near the Duke, putting herself in his way. "But I was sure my father spoke to you about me while he was with you."

"As I said, our business did not allow us time to discuss personal affairs. But you are forgetting your manners, are you not?" The Duke made to move around Lady Sophia. "I'm sure you cannot have forgotten Miss Darcy?"

"Of course." Lady Sophia and Georgiana exchanged only the most necessary courtesies before Lady Sophia said, "We have met once or twice since our initial introduction, have we not, Miss Darcy?"

Before Georgiana could answer, the Duke drew close to Lady Sophia and said in a hard voice, "Oh yes, I've heard about those meetings. You met at the Chocolatiere on Bond Street and again at church. Am I right?" The ladies were silent, but he required no response.

Georgiana tried to release his arm, mortified to be part of the confrontation, but he would not allow her to let go, choosing instead to lay his free hand over hers as it rested on his arm.

"Yes, Lady Sophia, I know all about your meetings. I would appreciate if, in the future, you were to keep family business, yours and most especially mine, a little more private." With that he left her standing in the corridor, visibly shaking, as he led Georgiana away. Elizabeth and Fitzwilliam followed close behind, both looking slightly scandalized by the exchange they had just witnessed.

There was quite a crowd filtering out of the galleries. The press grew thicker the closer they got to the cloak room, and Georgiana feared for her hem as she was buffeted and jostled from all sides. "Your Grace, I wish you would moderate your pace," she gasped as she struggled to keep up with his agitated stride.

"I am sorry, Miss Darcy. I had not realised I was walking so fast." His speech was rushed and he clenched his jaw, but he slowed down.

The Duke spotted a couple of vacant benches along the wall and changed direction. Georgiana and Elizabeth took a seat while the men stood nearby and waited for the throngs of people to clear.

Georgiana could not help but notice the frequent stares they were receiving from everyone who passed them. Men and women greeted the Duke amiably, but no one offered her or the Darcys a second glance unless it was one of contempt.

The Duke stood next to Georgiana with his hands clasped behind his back. Georgiana could see from the corner of her eye that his fingers were fidgeting, constantly tapping against the wall behind him with nervous energy. His movements were jerky and his eyes frequently scanned the crowd ahead of them.

"Your Grace, is something the matter?" Georgiana asked with genuine concern. Though she was not used to the open scorn so many were showing her, she would not allow herself to be affected by it, and she did not want it to hurt him either.

"No, Miss Darcy, I am well."

She did not believe him, though she questioned him no further. She wondered what the outcome of his trip to Abingdon had been and wondered that he had not spoken of it before now. She knew Lady Sophia had thought her father would offer her hand in marriage in exchange for allowing the Duke to keep Rothrage Manor, but it seemed as if the Marquess had not done so.

"I think the crowd has dispersed enough that we may call for my carriage without being trampled," the Duke said at length. "Shall we?" He offered his arm to Georgiana.

It rained a little harder on the return journey and the roads became very wet and muddy, but the Duke's carriage was well-sprung and delivered them home in safety. Once they pulled up in front of the Darcys' townhouse, they said their goodbyes in the carriage and dashed inside with the help of umbrella-wielding footmen.

Divested of their cloaks and bonnets, they went into the library and Fitzwilliam poured them all a glass of wine. He had not failed to notice the open hostility from several of the theatre patrons and, likewise, he had seen and understood the Duke's reaction. He was determined to discuss it with his sister.

Once Elizabeth and Georgiana were comfortably seated with their drinks he said, "Did you enjoy the opera, Georgiana?"

"I did, brother. Immensely."

"It was the same as last week. Pray tell, what made you enjoy tonight's performance so much more?" The brightest shade of red overspread Georgiana's face, neck, and chest as she sipped her wine and did not respond. "I am sure I can guess," Fitzwilliam continued. "It is that reason I want to address. I know Elizabeth has spoken to you in the past about the gentleman's attentions to you, but I think, in light of this week's events, we should readdress the topic. It is obvious to me His Grace likes you very much. Perhaps as much as I know you like him."

"No, brother, I assure you I do not—"

"It is useless to deny it, Georgiana. I am well aware of how you regard His Grace. I cannot fault you for your taste, dearest. He is an honest and kind man, but, as you saw this evening, nothing good will ever come from such a close association with him. I think tonight he realized it too."

A tear slipped from the corner of Georgiana's eye.

"I am sure you witnessed the cold looks and greetings we all received while in his presence. People whom we have called friends in the past were not able to look at us this evening without scorn. I think it is clear that the Ton sees our family's continued acquaintance with the Duke as officious. They are viewing you as a fortune hunter, dearest, and are scorning Elizabeth and myself because they believe we are encouraging you. Do you agree, Elizabeth?"

"I do." Elizabeth's words were spoken quietly, almost as if she feared saying them aloud.

"If the Duke comes for another visit, which he very well may not, I shall speak with him."

Georgiana's tears flowed freely now and she hiccupped on a sob.

"I know this is distressing to you, but, dearest, surely you saw how we were regarded this evening. I will not allow our family to be treated thusly, and I would not have people look poorly on His Grace, especially as he is such a good man. Please understand this is for your own good."

Georgiana set her glass of wine aside and wrapped her arms tight around her. "May I be excused?"

"Not yet. I need to make sure you are all right. I do not want a repeat of recent events."

Georgiana tightened her lips into a thin line. "I understand, Fitzwilliam. I shall be down to breakfast tomorrow."

"Very well, you may go to your room."

Without thanking him, without so much as a "good night" to either of them, Georgiana left the room, closing the door behind her. As soon as she heard the latch close, she broke into a run and did not stop until she reached her rooms. She gave Mary a terrific fright when she burst in and collapsed on her bed in tears. It took almost an hour of soothing, but at last Mary convinced her to remove her dress and put on her nightgown.

After Mary departed, Georgiana lay awake for hours, staring at the shadows that flickered across the ceiling from the fire in the grate.

Chapter Seventeen

Georgiana hardly slept that night; she was too distraught over all that her brother had said. She did not want to agree with him, though she knew he was right. How was she to explain that the Duke's company was worth more than anything and she would accept any criticism from the London Ton if it meant she could be near him? Her brother simply wouldn't understand.

She appeared cheerful enough when she went down to breakfast, but she declined to attend church, opting to remain at home and read excerpts from her prayer book. Fitzwilliam at first eyed her warily, but in the end consented and left her to her own devices.

Georgiana saw him and Elizabeth off and then retreated to the sitting room, settling in the window seat. Her prayer book remained closed in her lap while she watched the carriages and people on the street below. Reaching into the sleeve of her gown, she pulled out the Duke's handkerchief with the initials "DR" embroidered in the corner.

She had no notion of what the "D" stood for, but she knew the "R" stood for Rickords, the Duke's family name. She considered every name she could think of that began with the letter "D" until she fell asleep with her head propped on the windowpane.

When she awoke, a small pillow from the settee had been placed between her head and the hard pane. She quickly tucked the handkerchief away in her sleeve, afraid that whoever had put the pillow there may have noticed it in her hand while she slept. If her brother knew it was in her possession he would certainly demand she return it to the Duke.

She sat up straight, opened her prayer book, and resolutely applied herself to studying its contents. Half an hour later, Elizabeth and Fitzwilliam returned home in an agitated state. Elizabeth immediately began organizing the packing of the family's trunks and Fitzwilliam gave orders that the carriages were to be readied for their departure in the morning.

"Georgiana, go and ready your trunks," Fitzwilliam ordered as he passed her on the way to the library. "It is likely we will not be returning to London for quite some time, so take care to pack everything you value."

Georgiana followed him, a cold dread forming in the pit of her stomach. "Brother, what has happened? Why are we leaving in such haste?"

He did not answer, but went to his writing desk in the corner and began filling his satchel with every letter he could lay hands on.

"Brother—"

"Georgiana, go and pack your trunks immediately." His words were clipped and urgent.

"Brother, please," Georgiana begged, following Fitzwilliam to his study, here he began emptying the contents of the desk drawers into his satchel.

"I told you to pack your trunks. Go and do it now."

Though he spoke in harsh tones, she could tell he was not upset at her directly, but he was very angry and she knew it involved her somehow. "I will not. Not until you tell me what is going on."

Placing both hands on his desk, his shoulders tensed as he leaned over and stared Georgiana in the eyes. His eyes were wide and he had an almost wild appearance as he said, "I will repeat myself for the final time: go and pack your trunks. When everything is ready for our departure in the morning I may tell you, otherwise you shall hear on our trip northward when we have time to speak."

Georgiana gathered her resolve and, in a voice nowhere equal to her brothers, she fearfully said, "No, I shall not. I demand you tell me what is going on immediately. I know it has something to do with me. I deserve to know."

"You demand it." Fitzwilliam narrowed his eyes and stood straight. "Georgiana, you know you are not to question my authority. I am your guardian and I know what is best for you. If I say we leave London in the morning, then it is your duty to pack your trunks and be prepared to leave."

"You are not my only guardian. Richard is also

one. Perhaps I will choose to remain in London under his care."

"I shall send for Richard right now so that you may ask him, but I assure you he will not want you to remain in London and will support my decision to remove you."

"And, pray tell, why would he support you? You still have not told me why it is that we are to run away from London at a moment's notice. Perhaps if you trusted me with the details of my own life I may agree with you and run up and pack my trunks directly, but until you offer me some sort of explanation I am determined to refuse to do anything you say."

"When did you become so obstinate?" Fitzwilliam collapsed into the chair behind his desk and hung his head in his hands. "Very well, but I warn you it is not pleasant and you will wish it unsaid as soon as I speak the words."

Georgiana's mouth was dry as she took a seat in the chair across from her brother.

Scrubbing his hands over his face, he sat back and regarded her solemnly. "Do you know the extent of the previous rumours levelled at yourself and the Duke of Rothford?"

"I know we were accused of being found in a compromising position at the Harrisons' ball. I know we were accused of meeting clandestinely and without a chaperone. To own the truth, I am not exactly sure what the third accusation was."

"The third charge levelled at you was that you had lost your virtue to the Duke during one of the private meetings you were previously accused of."

"Oh, Lord!" She took a deep breath, swallowed, and then said, "I can only assume you heard of some new rumour today and you consider it even worse than these."

"I did and I do." Fitzwilliam's voice had lost its previous power. He sounded tired, defeated.

"How could it possibly be worse than the accusation that I lost my virtue to His Grace?"

"Trust me, dearest, it is worse. I would prefer you not know and take my word that we must leave London. Please, go to your rooms and pack your trunks. Let me take care of this."

"Tell me." She stared at her brother, making no move to rise from her chair. He looked at her with such sadness she almost changed her mind and begged him to be silent, but her need to know was greater than her fear, so she steeled herself to hear whatever he had to say.

"Today, while Elizabeth and I were at church, it was brought to our attention that all of London believes that you are the Duke of Rothford's mistress."

"His mistress!" Georgiana flinched at his words and sat deathly still. Hundreds of thoughts were racing through her mind, but she was unable to focus on any of them. At last, she raised her wide eyes to her brother's. Her breathing accelerated and she became very dizzy. She didn't speak. She didn't move. Fitzwilliam was at her side now, speaking to her, and his voice sounded as if he stood at the end of a long hallway. Georgiana could not comprehend a word he said. Her world began to spin and whirl out of control until she succumbed to blackness.

"*G*eorgiana, open your eyes." Fitzwilliam could not keep the worry from his voice. "Please, dearest. Wake up."

Georgiana forced her eyes to open for a moment before they fluttered closed again.

"That's it, open them again," he gently urged, rubbing her hand.

Georgiana felt a soft pillow slipped under her head, a cool cloth placed on her forehead, and heard the soft voice of Elizabeth. "There now, that should feel better."

Opening her eyes again, Georgiana noticed the anxious look on her brother's face, and asked, "What happened?"

"You fainted," he informed her in a tender voice.

"Fainted! But I've never fainted before."

"You've also never been under duress such as this before," Elizabeth reminded her.

"How long have I been unconscious?" she asked, realizing she was lying on the sofa in the study.

"Above a quarter of an hour," Fitzwilliam responded, clearly distressed over his sister's mental state.

"Do you think you can sit up?" Elizabeth asked as she brushed an errant curl off Georgiana's forehead.

Georgian pushed herself up to a sitting position with Elizabeth's help. The leather creaked under her as she sat. She bent her knees and drew legs close to her body, wrapping her arms around them. Resting her cheek on her knees, she closed her eyes against a small wave of dizziness.

Elizabeth rinsed the washcloth in the basin of water that sat on the floor nearby and wrung it out. "Here, place this on your neck. It should help a little."

Elizabeth laid the cool cloth on the back of Georgiana's neck and then sat on the edge of the couch next to her.

"I am a little overwhelmed, that's all."

"Fitzwilliam told you what we heard while we were at church today?"

"Yes. He did not want to, but I insisted. Do you also think we must leave London?"

"Do you not?" Elizabeth asked in surprise.

"Surely running away is not the best solution. Can His Grace not refute the rumour as he has the others?"

Fitzwilliam knelt at her side. "Georgiana, for some reason you and His Grace are being targeted by malicious persons, and until we determine who it is and why they persist on ruining you, we must leave London. We should have left long ago, but I had hoped it was all over. I should have known better and taken you to safety. Now, I fear, the rumours have gone too far."

"I am in agreement with your brother. Both you and His Grace have made no secret of your mutual regard. Though I believe him to be an honourable man, his conduct and yours, even amongst company, gives credence to this lie. Let us go to Pemberley and be done with this horrible affair. I am sure once you are out of London the rumourmongers will move on to the next unsuspecting target and leave you be."

"Very well, I shall go to my rooms and pack my things." Georgiana gave the wet cloth back to Elizabeth accepted her brother's hand to help her stand. "Fitzwilliam, I am sorry I was rude to you and did not do as I was told, but I am glad you told me."

"I accept your apology. You only wanted to know the truth. Off with you now; we leave in the morning, so you haven't much time to prepare your trunks."

Georgiana made her way to her rooms. Upon entering, she leaned against the door and bit the inside of her cheek to keep from crying. Her trunks were already brought up, and it looked as if Mary had begun to pack. One trunk was already filled with gowns. A second trunk lying open at the end of her bed was full of shoes, hats, gloves, shawls, cloaks, pelisses, and other outerwear. There were two more trunks at the side of the room completely empty. Georgiana moved towards them and, without calling Mary to help her, began to fill them herself. Every item she put away caused her more pain and grief.

Her favourite books lined one side of the trunk, a few fresh tears falling on their spines as she leaned over them. Her drawing supplies were organized in her drawing box and then packed beside the books. Her little box of keepsakes, her journal, and all of her letters were added to the trunk, each one causing her heart to wrench. This was her London diary. It never left the townhouse and usually remained locked in her desk. She had another at Pemberley. It could not stay now, for she may never return. Her heart cracked just a little when she closed the empty drawer of her desk and ran her hand over the mahogany.

She hardly noticed when Mary entered with an armful of freshly laundered chemises to resume her packing. The two worked in utter silence.

Her silver brush and mirror set was carefully wrapped and tucked down the side of the trunk so the glass would not be cracked. Collecting her jewellery, she placed it in the trunk with her gowns and then stood and looked around the room. Hours had passed since she had begun her task and, at last, she was finished. The trunks were taken downstairs and she sent Mary to bed, thanking her for a job well and swiftly done. Once she was alone, she gazed about her room, which looked so cold and strange, divested as it was of all her personal belongings. Collapsing onto her bed, Georgiana cried her last few remaining tears until she fell asleep.

Chapter Eighteen

$\mathcal{J}$t was very early when Georgiana woke to the sound of Mary moving about her room.

"Mary, what time is it?" Georgiana asked, sitting up. She had slept in her clothes from the night before. A thick quilt had been placed over her to keep her warm.

"It is six o'clock, miss. Your brother wishes to leave no later than eight o'clock. He wants to be outside of London before the streets become too crowded. Breakfast is being laid out as we speak. Would you like to dress now?"

"Yes, Mary, that is fine."

Georgiana went about her morning ablutions and changed into her carriage dress before going down to breakfast. When she arrived in the breakfast room, Elizabeth was already there. "Come eat, Georgiana. Cook has laid out a wonderful assortment of cold meats, cheese, bread, and fruit."

"Where is Fitzwilliam?"

"He is having a word with Mr. Grey and shall return in a few minutes."

Georgiana filled her plate and took a seat next to Elizabeth. Fitzwilliam entered soon after and accepted the plate Elizabeth made for him. They both looked tired. Georgiana supposed they had been up all night writing letters and overseeing the packing of the household and giving orders as to what should be taken now and what should follow them after they departed. It was clear neither anticipated the family returning to London for a very long time.

Georgiana had made her own preparations last night for taking leave of the London staff, praying all the while that her absence might be a short one after all. "Fitzwilliam, if you will excuse me, I would like to take my leave of Mrs. Grey and Cook."

"Very well. Do not tarry overlong. We leave as planned at eight."

"I will be ready." Georgiana made her way downstairs and tearfully said goodbye to the housekeeper and cook she had known and loved her entire life. They were both well aware of the London gossip, and even though they knew they would not see Georgiana for a very long time, they were glad her brother was taking her away. She would be better off at Pemberley, and they had no doubt Mrs. Reynolds would take good care of her.

"Please accept this as a token of my appreciation for all you've done for me," Georgiana said, pressing a small parcel into each lady's hand.

"Miss Darcy, you didn't have to give us anything,"

Mrs. Grey said, pulling her into an embrace.

"I wanted to. I will miss you both so much." Georgiana reached out and clasped Cook's hand while still embracing Mrs. Grey. Cook wasn't one for displays of affection, but Georgiana loved her and wanted her to know it. Cook, stoic as ever, said nothing as she gave Georgiana a little box of biscuits.

The carriage with the family's trunks had been sent on its way to Longbourn, where they planned to stop for the children, half an hour before the Darcys had boarded their travel carriage. A third carriage, much smaller and less grand, followed with their lady's maids and Fitzwilliam's valet.

The ride to Longbourn was almost twenty-five miles. Though it was normally a very pleasant ride full of conversation, this was not the case today. They were far too overcome to speak to one another.

When at last the carriage arrived at Longbourn Mr. and Mrs. Bennet came rushing out of the house to greet them. Little Jane was in Mrs. Bennet's arms, bundled in blankets against the cold, and Bennet trotted on the heels of his grandfather.

"Papa!" Bennet yelled as soon as a footman opened the carriage door. No sooner were Fitzwilliam's feet on the ground than Bennet was wrapped around his legs.

Fitzwilliam swept his son into his arms and hugged him. The footman helped Elizabeth and Georgiana out of the carriage and instantly Elizabeth rushed over to join the merry reunion with the children she had missed so dearly.

Jane began to wiggle and coo in her grandmother's arms and Mrs. Bennet had to hand her over to Elizabeth for fear of dropping the dear girl.

"Elizabeth, my dear, how good it is to see you. Oh, give me a kiss!" Mrs. Bennet could hardly contain her excitement; she was almost as giddy as the children. "Come in, come in! We'll catch our death of cold out here. Let us go in where it is warm and have tea. You must be frozen through after your journey. What a pleasure it is to have you here! I was sure your carriage would be overturned in the mud and you'd all be killed."

As they made their way inside, Mrs. Bennet continued to chatter pleasantly about the many ways the Darcys could have met their demise on the road from London. Georgiana, always overwhelmed by the woman's effusiveness, hardly heard a word. She was stiff and cold from the long ride and still much depressed in spirit. A cup of tea and her nephew's affectionate kisses went a long way towards restoring her.

Bennet settled down once the adults were all seated by the fire with cups of steaming tea. He took a tea biscuit and sat at the little table by the window. Elizabeth beamed at her son as she cuddled Jane on her lap. "He is such a good boy. How I missed him and Jane while we were away. I hope they weren't any trouble for you, Mama."

"Trouble? How could you even think such a

thing? They were no trouble at all. Your father took Bennet on nature walks or went fishing at least twice a week while the weather was warm. Thick as thieves, the two of them. And my Miss Jane"—Mrs. Bennet leaned forward and tickled Jane under the chin—"is an angel."

Jane looked up and cooed at her grandmamma. Mrs. Bennet tore off a little piece of her tea biscuit and gently fed it to her.

"Mama, Jane is very young; be careful with the size of the pieces you give her."

"I know, Elizabeth. I raised five daughters, remember?" Mrs. Bennet turned her attention back to Jane, breaking off another piece of the biscuit. "Do not forget Jane has spent much of the spring here with us. She loves biscuits." Mrs. Bennet nuzzled Jane, making her giggle.

Elizabeth smiled at her mother's antics. With all five of her daughters married, Mrs. Bennet had become the epitome of the doting grandmother to all six of her grandchildren. She was unable to see her elder daughters' children as often as she might wish, for the Bingleys had given up Netherfield some time ago and purchased an estate in Derbyshire near Pemberley, but as her younger daughters had both married local men she was able to dote on Mary's daughter and Kitty's son quite thoroughly.

"Miss Darcy, it is very good to see you," Mrs. Bennet said, remembering her place as hostess. "I must say you look more beautiful each time I see you."

"Thank you, Mrs. Bennet."

"What are your plans? How long do you intend to stay?" Mr. Bennet asked Fitzwilliam.

"Just one night. I'm afraid we must be on our way to Pemberley tomorrow."

"I am glad you will stay the night," Mrs. Bennet said, "for I sent word to my sister Phillips that I would bring Jane by this afternoon for one last visit before you whisked her away to Derbyshire. She simply adores her grandniece. I have also sent notes to Mary and Kitty and invited their families to dinner. Just think, four of my grandchildren together! Elizabeth, will an hour give you and Miss Darcy enough time to refresh yourselves before we go into Meryton?"

Elizabeth had no desire to go scampering about Meryton with her mother, but she knew there would be no refusing her. Judging from the resigned look on Georgiana's face, her sister-in-law knew it too. "Yes, Mama."

Their first stop was at the home of Mrs. Phillips. Elizabeth watched closely for any sign the woman had heard of the rumours from town, but as far as she could tell her aunt treated Georgiana no differently than she ever had. The woman was far too busy fussing over little Jane and asserting how miserable she would be without her little angel to pay Georgiana more attention beyond her proper greeting. This eased Elizabeth's troubled mind greatly.

Mrs. Bennet lingered at her sister's door with

baby Jane while Mrs. Phillips said her prolonged goodbyes. Elizabeth and Georgiana went ahead, and as they crossed the street to visit Mary they came upon Lady Lucas exiting one of the apartments over a shop.

"Mrs. Darcy, I did not know you were in Meryton," she said, casting a wary glance at Georgiana. She did not speak to the young woman or offer her any greeting. "I was just visiting my friend, Mrs. Jones."

"It is a pleasure to see you, Lady Lucas. And how is Mrs. Jones?" Elizabeth asked, watching her just as warily as she watched Georgiana.

"As well as can be expected. She is always poorly this time of year. The damp, you see, gets in her bones. She was able to take some of the broth I brought her, so I hope she shall improve soon."

"It is very kind of you to take such care of her."

"But what brings you to Meryton?" She looked at Georgiana out of the corner of her eye a second time. "I had thought you would remain in London for the entire season."

"We are passing through on our way to Pemberley. Urgent business calls Mr. Darcy home immediately. Georgiana and I did not like to remain in town without him."

"Yes, well, if you will excuse me, I must be on my way. Give my regards to your mother."

Lady Lucas scurried off with undue haste, casting almost fearful glances behind her.

"Do you think the people of Meryton have heard the rumours?" Georgiana asked with a tremor of worry in her voice.

Elizabeth frowned. "If I were to hazard a guess based on Lady Lucas's behaviour, I would have to say yes, the knowledge is widespread. But here comes my mother. Let us see how Mary receives us."

Mary was already at the door when they approached. She supported her daughter on her right hip. Her rigid posture was all too familiar to Elizabeth and she immediately tensed for the lecture she knew was brewing. Cautiously, she approached her younger sister. "Mary, it is good to see you." Elizabeth clasped Mary's hand and smiled at her daughter. "Look at how much Margaret has grown. I can hardly recognize her."

Georgiana approached behind Elizabeth and Mary's already stern manner became severe. "I am sorry, but I cannot allow my daughter to be exposed to persons who wholly disregard propriety and engage in immoral and sinful behaviour. My husband and I have discussed it and we agree that Miss Darcy is no longer welcome in our home. I am afraid I must ask you to leave."

Never had anyone, even Lady Sophia Beck, treated Georgiana in such a discourteous and abusive manner.

"Mary," Elizabeth snapped, "surely you do not believe the vicious rumours which have been spread about Miss Darcy in London?"

"In my experience, rumours generally have some basis in truth," Mary stiffly responded. "Even if Miss Darcy did not commit the acts she has been charged with, she has done something to raise suspicion. What that is I know not, nor do I care. We have made our decision and your sister is not welcome in our home." Without another word, Mary entered her house and shut the door behind her.

"Come, Elizabeth, let us go home," said a very shocked and upset Mrs. Bennet. She had her arm around Georgiana, who was so distraught that she was hardly able to get air. She was soon gasping and Elizabeth waved for the carriage to come for them immediately.

The driver wasted no time in avoiding all of the ruts and potholes as he typically did on the return trip to Longbourn, but his passengers were much too upset to notice the bumpiness of the ride. Mrs. Bennet had her hands full trying to appease her mewling granddaughter, who was frightened by Georgiana's emotional outburst. Elizabeth cradled Georgiana in her arms while her slender body was wracked with sobs.

Mr. Darcy came out of the library when the carriage pulled up. He thought to steal his daughter away for a moment or two before her nurse or grandmother reclaimed her. His plans changed, however, as soon as his wife, sister, daughter, and mother-in-law all stepped into the foyer.

"What is it? What has happened?" Fitzwilliam demanded as he rushed to his wife and sister.

Georgiana's sobs became louder and harder, and once again she was gasping for air. Elizabeth tried to calm her while Mrs. Bennet recounted the confrontation at Mary's house. Fitzwilliam was furious, determined to ride into Meryton and demand an apology. Elizabeth forestalled him, insisting that he stay and help calm his sister. He would be of more use to her here than he would be by running off to remonstrate with the sanctimonious Mary.

They took Georgiana to Elizabeth's old room and tried everything from smelling salts to brandy to calm her, but she was inconsolable. Elizabeth was just about to resort to laudanum when at last she exhausted herself and fell asleep upon the bed.

Elizabeth and Fitzwilliam tiptoed out of the room and instructed Georgiana's lady's maid to sit outside the door and call them if she was heard again.

Downstairs, Mrs. Bennet had informed her husband of all that had transpired in Meryton and he was almost as furious as Fitzwilliam.

"How is she?" he asked as soon as they settled in the drawing room.

"I have never seen her so distressed," Fitzwilliam responded. The worry etched in the lines of his face made him appear ten years older. "I fear her fine spirit has been broken. She is sleeping now, and I pray she finds peace and comfort in it."

"That feeble-minded, unfeeling girl! We should have taken better care in her upbringing." Mr. Bennet pinched the bridge of his nose with his thumb and forefinger. "How could anyone who knows Miss Darcy, especially those in this family, believe such heinous lies? Never, not once, did Mrs. Bennet and I give credit to them."

"Thank you, Papa, that means the world to us to hear you say that," Elizabeth said.

Though Mr. and Mrs. Bennet had heard of the London gossip, they did not know the full extent of it. The Darcys informed them, and then Mr. and Mrs. Bennet disclosed the few bits of information they had gleaned from their neighbours over the past month. The day's events and the Bennets' disclosures only assured Fitzwilliam he was doing the right thing by removing his family to Pemberley.

Chapter Nineteen

A note was dispatched to Kitty explaining why the family dinner party was cancelled. Her reply was short but heartfelt: she was sorry to miss the chance to see her sister's family, and Georgiana was welcome in her home at any time, especially if she should need spiritual counsel. Since being removed from Lydia's influence, Kitty had steadily improved in character; now that she had married a clergyman and taken on the mantles of wife and mother, she nearly rivalled her eldest sister in sweet-tempered goodness. Moved by Kitty's sincerity, Fitzwilliam resolved to secure for her husband a valuable living near Pemberley. The man who could work such a change in a formerly selfish, attention-seeking girl could do a great deal of good for a larger flock than he shepherded at present.

No one had much of an appetite that evening, and so a light supper was served in lieu of dinner. They had just returned to the drawing room when there was a knock on the front door.

"Who could it be at this hour? It's almost nine o'clock," Mrs. Bennet said, straining to see out the darkened window.

A moment later, Mrs. Hill scurried into the room. "His Grace the Duke of Rothford is here. He sends you his card, Ma'am." Mrs. Hill held out a small silver tray with the Duke's calling card.

Mrs. Bennet snatched it up and gazed at it in wonder. "A duke! In my house, Lord bless me! Oh, what fine paper he uses!" She turned it over and read the note scribbled on the back. "He apologises for the lateness of the hour and begs my leave to see Mr. Darcy. A duke! Begging my leave! Good heavens! As if I should dare to refuse him!"

Fitzwilliam exchanged confused glances with Elizabeth. "Mr. Bennet, may I use your library to speak with His Grace?"

"Of course, anything you need," Mr. Bennet answered.

Mr. Darcy left the room. A moment later, the distinct bass voice of the Duke of Rothford was heard in the foyer greeting Fitzwilliam.

The pair had been sequestered in the library for three quarters of an hour when Elizabeth excused herself to check on Georgiana. Mary reported no sounds or movements from within. Upon opening the door a crack and peeking in with a candle, Elizabeth was surprised to see Georgiana's eyes were open.

"You are awake," Elizabeth said, coming into the room. She set the candle on the bedside table and sat on the edge of the bed.

"I heard a carriage in the drive some time ago. Have the Bennets more company?"

"Yes, a rather late caller." Georgiana made no response. "Would you not care to know who it is?"

"Why should I care? It is not likely anyone in Meryton would want to see me."

"Just because one person was vicious does not make them all so. I think you will want to know who is here."

"Very well, you may tell me."

"His Grace the Duke of Rothford."

Georgiana sat up so suddenly that she felt giddy. "He is here, at Longbourn?"

"Yes, he is with your brother in the library."

"What is he doing here?"

"I do not know, but I am sure your brother will tell us as soon as their meeting is concluded. How do you feel?"

"I am still distressed, but I will not fly into hysterics again if that is what you are asking."

"I am glad to hear it. Are you hungry? I can have Mrs. Hill send up a tray."

"No, I do not think I could eat anything, but thank you for thinking of me."

"Of course."

"Lizzy, I would like to go downstairs so I can see the Duke before he leaves."

"Georgie, I don't think that's a good idea."

"Why not?" Georgiana questioned.

"In truth, dearest, you look dreadful. It has been a very long day and you need your rest after such a shock. I will go down and give His Grace your regard if you wish, but I would like you to stay where you are."

Georgiana's protest was interrupted by a barely perceptible knock on the door. Elizabeth got up to answer it.

"What is it, Fitzwilliam," Elizabeth asked when she saw her husband on the other side.

"His Grace wonders if Georgiana is well enough to speak with him tonight or if she prefers to see him in the morning." His voice was low as he was afraid of waking his sister.

"The morning!" Elizabeth exclaimed. "Will His Grace be staying in Meryton tonight?"

"No, he will be staying here at Longbourn. Your mother is making sure the best rooms are ready for him as we speak. Do not be surprised if she gives him our rooms." A small smile graced his lips as he said it.

"Come in and ask her yourself; she is awake. I have no doubt what her answer will be. She has already expressed her desire to go down and see him."

Elizabeth swept the door open and allowed Fitzwilliam entrance. Georgiana was still sitting up on the bed, her eyes shining.

"Dearest, would you—"

"Yes, tell His Grace I will be down in half an hour."

"You did not even hear what I have to say."

"I heard you tell Elizabeth." Throwing the blanket off her lap, she climbed out of bed. She had been entirely too upset earlier to change out of her visiting dress or let down her hair. Her skirts were hopelessly wrinkled and her hairpins had abandoned their positions. With her red eyes and puffy lids, she truly looked a fright. "I shall just change my dress and tidy my hair before coming down. Elizabeth, will you aide me?"

Elizabeth sighed and nodded, shooing her husband out the door to entertain His Grace while he waited. Mary was called in, and together they worked quickly to make Georgiana presentable. By the time she descended the stairs, the physical toll of the day's events was only visible if one looked closely.

Time seemed to move slowly as she put one foot in front of the other, and yet before she knew it she was stepping into the drawing room. The Duke jumped to his feet and bowed upon her entrance. His brown eyes staring into hers caused her stomach to flip and her knees to tremble. Georgiana took a seat on the chair opposite him and said, "Your Grace, what a surprise it is to see you here."

"It is almost as much a surprise to me as it is to you. I hope your journey here was pleasant."

"Yes, the roads were quite dry this morning. We made very good time in coming."

"I am glad to hear it. Miss Darcy, would you do me the honour of speaking with me in the library?"

Georgiana's stomach flipped once more at this request for a private interview. She looked to her brother for permission and, to her astonishment, he nodded his approval. "Of course, Your Grace."

Her thoughts scrambled madly on the short walk

to the library. What could this signify? What could the Duke have to say to her that her family could not hear? Torn between hope and dread, she took a seat on the sofa in Mr. Bennet's cosy library and the Duke boldly took a seat next to her.

He did not speak for a long time. Desperate to fill the awkward silence, Georgiana blurted, "Did you have trouble finding Longbourn?"

"I did not have trouble finding the place once I knew of it, but I had a devil of a time discovering where you had gone. When I went to call on you today I was informed by Mr. Grey that you had quit London entirely. I had to threaten the man to get even that much out of him."

"Do not blame him," Georgiana pleaded. "My brother told him not to inform anyone of our departure or our destination."

"Yes, well, he is a most devoted servant. I'll wager the Regent himself does not have such dedicated men."

"He is only trying to protect me. Mr. and Mrs. Grey have been with my family for decades. They are devoted to our well-being and have been quite distressed about the gossip circulating London. If I am allowed to surmise, not even your threats made Mr. Grey give up our whereabouts. I am more likely to believe you said something in my defence to sway him."

"You know him well, Miss Darcy."

"What is it that you said to gain Mr. Grey's trust?"

"Oh, you give me too much credit, and him not enough. He still refused to tell me anything other than that you had left London. I had to seek out your cousin to learn you were to return to Pemberley, and even then I travelled to Luton and back before finding you here. I knew I should have overtaken you before you reached Luton, but when I did not I sent men to every inn and learned you had not come that far yet. One splendid innkeeper took pity on me and told me that Mr. Darcy had married a woman from the neighbourhood of Meryton and I might have better luck there. And so, through providence, here I am."

The Duke looked at Georgiana for a long time before continuing. "I was very distressed when I called on you today only to learn you had left London."

"Yes, well, we thought it best under the circumstances."

"I cannot blame your brother for taking you away, but I do blame all of London for their vicious lies. It pains me that you were hurt again."

"That is very kind of you, Your Grace."

"It is not kind of me, it is selfish." The Duke stood and paced in front of the fire for a moment before turning to gaze adoringly at Georgiana. "Miss Darcy, this morning when I woke I had the uncontrollable urge to see you. I had thought to be no more than a friend to you, a patron of sorts to help you in society, but something unforeseen has happened."

A feeling of breathlessness swept over Georgiana at his words. Coming closer, the Duke knelt before her, took her hands in his, and raised them to his lips. As he kissed her hands, heat surged up her arms, setting her heart afire.

"I tried to imagine you as a sister, a niece, as someone out of my reach. Instead I found myself imagining you as Duchess of Rothrage Castle, pushing our future children on the tree-swing in the west gardens, just as my mother did for my brothers and me when we were small. Miss Darcy, do you understand what I am saying?"

She was too breathless to answer him, but he appeared to take no notice as he continued. "I was made to love you forever. There, I finally gathered the strength to tell you. I can pretend I do not need you, that I do not want to be with you, but I would be fooling myself. You are the one I have been dreaming of my entire life. You are the one I have been looking for, the one I have been waiting for. When I close my eyes, I see your face. I will never be happy until we are together. Miss Darcy, will you do me the greatest honour and consent to be my wife?"

Georgiana was aglow with the warmth of happiness as she gazed at him. "Your Grace, when the scandalous gossip spread around London, I feared I would never find my one true love. I despaired of ever finding happiness in marriage. Then I met you, and I knew my fears were all unfounded. For weeks I have loved you, and with every day that passes I feel I love you more. Yes, I will be your wife, and I will love you forever."

He kissed her hands again, more fervently this time, and then reached up to touch a silky curl at the nape of her neck.

She had not intended to, but she could not help

leaning forward and pressing her soft lips against his. She had never kissed a man and had not known what to expect. She certainly had not expected the swirls of emotions that coursed through her. His lips were a searing fire against hers as he returned her kiss. When she pulled away, the fire dwindled to smouldering embers that longed to re-ignite. Pressing her hand to her heaving chest, she tried to catch her breath. He had stolen it yet again.

She took a moment to compose herself, then asked, "What does the 'D' in your initials stand for?"

"Devin."

"Devin," she repeated, savouring the sound.

"My God, Georgiana, it sounds like heaven coming from your lips." His voice was husky, choked with emotion. Oh, how she loved it! "I shall speak to your brother immediately."

Chapter Twenty

Upon opening the door, Georgiana found her brother and Elizabeth standing at the end of the hall waiting for them. Fitzwilliam was clearly agitated and Elizabeth was trying to calm him. The radiance of Georgiana's countenance told Elizabeth all she needed to know. She rushed to her sister-in-law, clasping her hands.

"Mr. Darcy, may I speak to you, sir?" the Duke of Rothford asked formally.

"Of course, Your Grace."

Fitzwilliam followed him into the library. As soon as the library door closed, Georgiana looked at Elizabeth and said, "Oh, Lizzy, I am so happy! He loves me and asked me to marry him. I have accepted him."

"I am so happy for you," Elizabeth said. "I am sure your brother is accepting him; he told me he would. Come, let us wait for them in the drawing room."

Mrs. Bennet was still upstairs with Mrs. Hill, preparing the best rooms in the house for the Duke, taking care to stoke his fire, prepare enough hot water, and provide him extra blankets in case he should need them. She was just coming down when the men finished their conversation. It was well past eleven o'clock when at last the Duke requested introductions to Mrs. Bennet. Mr. Bennet he had already met while he waited for Georgiana to come down.

He offered her his most gracious bow and his thanks for being accepted into her home. He promised he would never again intrude without invitation, and Mrs. Bennet likewise promised he could arrive at any time, day or night, and she would be happy to have him as her guest.

The couple's happy announcement was made known to Mr. and Mrs. Bennet, who promised not to breathe a word until it was made public. They offered their congratulations to the couple and welcomed the Duke into their family. Mrs. Bennet could not wait until she could tell her sister that there was *almost* a duke in the family.

The Duke resolved to return to London. He was certain an announcement in the papers and a few well-placed words would clear up the latest rumours about Georgiana being his mistress. He could not stop the Ton from labelling her an ambitious title seeker, but he vowed none would dare do so in his presence. He was also confident he had determined the source of the rumours and was set on a confrontation to learn the truth.

Though Fitzwilliam also had business in town, he thought it best to keep his family at Longbourn for the time being. He wrote a letter of instruction to his cousin, which the Duke would carry with him. If all went well, he was to return in two days, after which the Darcys would continue on to Pemberley. The duke planned to join them. Their luggage was sent for so that the ladies might refresh their wardrobes, and everyone settled in to wait.

On the day she expected His Grace to return, Georgiana took special care with her appearance. Mary styled her hair in an intricate French coiffure that Mrs. Bennet had never seen the likes of before. Her prettiest dresses were laid out for the day and she sat by the window to keep an almost constant vigil.

It was all for naught, and she slept ill that night wondering why the Duke had not returned. The following morning she repeated her preparations, and again she was disappointed when he did not return.

Five days passed and still the Duke had not returned, nor had any letter been received from him or from Richard. Georgiana was in quite a state. Every day she watched the papers for the engagement announcement which had yet to appear.

After breakfast, she begged her brother to ride to London and find out the reason for the delay. "Please, Fitzwilliam, you must go. What if something has happened to him? What if he has taken a fall from his horse and been injured?"

"Georgiana, do be serious. I am sure it is just that his business has taken longer than he expected."

"Why has he not sent word, then?"

"Perhaps he is not used to informing others when his plans change. I am certain it is just a small oversight."

"What about Richard, why has he not written?"

"Dearest, calm yourself. No doubt we will hear from him soon."

However, the following morning when the Duke still had not returned and there was no letter from Richard, Fitzwilliam had to confess even he was beginning to wonder what was causing the delay. He did not know the Duke that well and could not begin to guess his reasoning, but the same could not be said for his cousin. Truly, Richard's continued silence was most perplexing.

"I think I will go to London today," Fitzwilliam announced at breakfast.

"At last," Georgiana said. "Thank you, brother. You must know how distressed I am." She was indeed; the dark circles around her eyes were a testament to her lack of sleep, and her complexion was pale and drawn. "Please, hurry your return and, if possible, bring His Grace with you."

Georgiana and Elizabeth had expected Fitzwilliam to return that night, for London was only twenty-five miles and the ride on horseback could easily be accomplished in a matter of hours with only one stop to rest the horse. He did not return; in his place he sent a letter by express.

He assured them both he and the Duke were well, but that he would remain in London with the Duke to clear up some business. Richard also sent his apologies for neglecting to write, claiming he had been far too busy. It was apparent something else had happened, but the letter gave them no additional clues.

The following day a second letter arrived containing much the same information as the first: the men were well and still detained by business. At least her brother was writing regularly, even if his missives lacked any information of substance. They knew the men were safe, and that was something.

This continued for three more days. Georgiana was a bundle of nerves. Elizabeth refused to let her go into Meryton and chose to remain at Longbourn herself.

At last, on Thursday, there in the society pages of the London Times was the announcement that Miss Georgiana Darcy of Pemberley would marry His Grace the seventh Duke of Rothford. The announcement was large and took up a quarter of the page with the engagement details.

"May I keep it?" Georgiana asked Mr. Bennet when he showed it to her.

"Of course." He first looked at the other side to make sure there was nothing he should like to read and then tore out the announcement and handed it to her.

"Elizabeth, do you think Fitzwilliam and His Grace will return today?"

"Perhaps," she said, though she had no idea whether they would or not.

They did not return, but once again another express

came, this time with two letters, one for Elizabeth and another for Georgiana.

Georgiana ran straight to her room and closed the door before breaking the seal. She devoured the letter, taking in every word her fiancé had written. His letter was not long, telling her he would return tomorrow and declaring how much he missed her. He closed by sending his love and expressing his desire that they would marry soon. Georgiana wished the letter was a little longer, but she could not fault how much sincere emotion he had squeezed into so few words.

That night she slept a little better knowing her beloved would soon return to her after ten days of separation. Like she had more than a week ago, she awoke with energy and took great care in dressing and styling her hair. No sooner had she gone down to breakfast than horses were heard coming up the drive. The gentlemen had returned.

Elizabeth went directly to Fitzwilliam to greet him when he stepped into the foyer, and Georgiana did the same to the Duke.

The Duke cocked a half smile and stepped close. Clasping both of her hands in his, he kissed her fingertips, settled their combined hands against his chest, and looked intently at her face. "At last, I get to see you again."

"I would scold you for being away for so long, but after your greeting I find I cannot," she said, looking up at him.

A rakish smile overspread his face. He glanced at her brother, who was still greeting Elizabeth. Then he brushed his lips against Georgiana's and pulled back quickly, hoping no one had seen.

Georgiana's cheeks flamed with colour at his boldness. She longed for the opportunity to speak to him in private, but Fitzwilliam and Elizabeth were moving deeper into the house and they were expected to follow.

No one ate until the gentlemen were refreshed and able to join them for breakfast, which took no more than half an hour as they were most desirous to be with the ladies and the early start to their journey had left them quite hungry. Mr. Darcy assured the Duke there were no secrets with his wife's family and that they could be trusted, so the whole of the story was laid out before them over breakfast.

"When I returned to London I found a letter on my desk," the Duke began. "My butler informed me it had arrived that very morning. The letter directed me to pay a sum of twenty thousand pounds or the blackmailer would continue to malign the characters of Miss Darcy and myself." He rubbed his forehead as he remembered the distress the letter had caused him. "I immediately called upon your cousin, Colonel Fitzwilliam, for assistance. You see, I had pieced together a theory regarding Lady Sophia Beck and her association with Captain George Wickham."

"Good God, what does he have to do with this?" Mr. Bennet exclaimed. He was never pleased to hear mention of his least favourite son-in-law. Mrs. Bennet sat quietly in her seat with wide eyes, for once unable to say anything.

"Perhaps I should start from the beginning," the Duke said with a wry smile. "Upon the death of my father, I learned that Rothrage Manor, one of the largest estates in my duchy, was to transfer to the Marquess of Mardsen. My father had not been in his right mind for some time before his death, and Lord Mardsen, who was fully aware of my father's diminished capacity, manipulated him into making a most foolish wager. I have, of course, contested the validity of the wager and accused the man of taking advantage of my sickly father.

"The Marquess intended to give Rothrage Manor to his younger son, Lieutenant Beck, who would then be able to give up his military commission entirely. The Lieutenant promised his friend, Captain Wickham, that he would give him the position of steward over the estate once he took possession. The two organized leave from their regiments and came to London. They did not foresee that I would not directly hand over the estate and instead choose to contest the wager. Lieutenant Beck quickly became desperate, as he had already burned many bridges in his military career and felt he could not return at the end of his leave. He turned to his sister, Lady Sophia, for help.

"It is Lady Sophia's greatest ambition to be Duchess of Rothrage. She had missed her chance with my older brother, and when I refused her hand she, too, became desperate. She and her brother concocted a plan which they hoped would secure both their futures. They would embark upon a campaign of character assassination and blackmail in order to force me to accede to their wishes.

"Their first step in this plan was to associate me in a scandal with a lady of society."

"And this is where George Wickham made himself useful, is it?" Mr. Bennet interjected sourly.

"Yes it is. Captain Wickham told his friend he knew just the lady to target, one who had nearly been involved in scandal before, one whose brother would do anything and pay any amount to protect her. To his dubious credit, Captain Wickham was only peripherally involved, providing no more than Georgiana's name and part of her history with him. The rest came from Lady Sophia and Lieutenant Beck. The two of them hoped to drive me into a corner. With my character ruined, my legal suit against Lord Mardsen would likely be dismissed and no reputable lady would have me. I would lose the estate and be forced to marry Lady Sophia to restore my good name. Or so they wished me to believe.

"By extraordinary luck on her part, Lady Sophia witnessed a chance encounter between myself and Georgiana outside the library at the Harrisons' ball and knew her moment had come to strike. When neither Georgiana nor I acted according to their plan, the conspirators grew even more desperate, Lady Sophia especially. She lashed out personally at Georgiana, trying to drive her away, and even turned on her brother by begging her father to offer the estate in exchange for agreeing to marry her—a plan which her father staunchly rejected. Her actions created a schism between herself and her brother, and he took up with Captain Wickham once again to carry out a new plan, which brings me back to the blackmail letter."

"What exactly did the letter say?" Georgiana wondered aloud.

"As I said before, it demanded I pay twenty thousand pounds or a certain event in your past would be revealed to the public."

Georgiana knew exactly what he referred to. She was glad she had been the one to tell him of her history with Wickham rather than him learning about it in such an odious manner.

"Though the letter was unsigned, I was confident I had pieced together where the threats were coming from," the Duke continued. "And so, with the help of Mr. Darcy and Colonel Fitzwilliam, we tracked the men to their hiding place and apprehended them. It was then that the Lieutenant confessed the entire scheme."

"What has happened to them?" Mrs. Bennet asked hesitantly. She was deeply concerned for Lydia, who had always been her favourite.

"Lieutenant Beck and Captain Wickham were arrested on charges of desertion and attempted blackmail. You see, neither of the men returned to their regiment at the conclusion of their leave."

"Oh, my dear Lydia!" Mrs. Bennet cried, bursting into tears. "Mr. Wickham is sure to be court marshalled, and then he will be hanged, and then what will become of our dear girl?"

"Calm yourself, my dear," Mr. Bennet said with his

usual aplomb. "Perhaps he will only be transported." Mrs. Bennet's wails grew louder and Mr. Bennet sighed. "There, there, do not distress yourself. Lydia shall come home to us, if we can manage it. Perhaps her grave misfortune will teach her sobriety. But please continue, Your Grace. What of the Marquess of Mardsen?"

"Although we were unable to level charges against the Marquess, who was not part of the scheme, the actions of his children have hurt his case considerably. He has accepted payment in lieu of the title and Rothrage Manor is once again my brother's estate during his lifetime."

"I am glad to hear it," Georgiana said, beaming up at him.

"You will also be happy to know that a public apology will appear in Monday's society section of the London Times from the Marquess on behalf of his son, and our reputations are free and clear of all scandal. You may return at any time without fear of being shunned."

"Now I shall receive disapproving looks for an entirely different reason," Georgiana said.

"Why is that?" he asked curiously.

"Because I am marrying far above my station in life."

"All you must do is tell me when someone looks down on you and I shall take care of it. You will be the Duchess of Rothford; no one has the right to look disapprovingly at you ever again."

Chapter Twenty-One

The wedding of Miss Georgiana Darcy and the Duke of Rothford was set for the twenty-fifth of June. The event was all anyone in London could talk about. The Darcys returned to London to purchase Georgiana's trousseau and then hosted one of the largest dinner parties London had ever seen. Everyone who was anyone was invited, and they eagerly returned to town from the country for the event.

It was a rousing success. Those of the Duke's friends who had doubted Georgiana's intentions came away absolutely charmed and convinced of her goodness and her real affection for her fiancé. Those of Georgiana's friends and family who had feared the Duke would be haughty found him quite amiable and approachable. After six extravagant courses and the best port to be had in London, there wasn't a person in the house who would allow a bad word to be said of either the Duke or his future bride.

"Mrs. Darcy, you are a fine hostess," the Duke

said as he was taking his leave. "Thank you for organising such a splendid gathering on our behalf. After tonight, the whole of London will want you to plan their dinner parties."

"Thank you, Your Grace, it was my pleasure." Elizabeth smiled and curtsied while Fitzwilliam clasped hands and told him to have a good evening.

"Miss Darcy, will you walk me out?" the Duke asked, offering Georgiana his arm. They lingered in the foyer to say their goodbyes. Mr. Grey and the footman had the good sense to remain at their posts with their eyes averted, though the couple's behaviour was entirely proper.

"You should know that you are my life now. Everything I do is done with you in my thoughts," he whispered as he bent over her hand to kiss it. Not giving her time to respond, he strode down the steps and then glanced back at her before stepping into his carriage. He was well out of sight around the corner before Georgiana stepped out of the doorway and allowed Mr. Grey to close the door behind her.

That night after retiring to her room, Georgiana lay on her bed thinking of her last few remaining days as a single woman. She fell asleep with a smile on her face as she considered how happy she would be as Devin's wife.

*G*eorgiana had been too swept up in her wedding preparations to notice how her brother was holding up, but when she came down to breakfast the day before they were to depart for Abingdon for the wedding she recognised the strain in his features.

"Brother, are you well?"

Sitting up straight, he cleared his throat. "I am well, dearest. How are you?"

"I couldn't be better. His Grace will be arriving with a carriage today. Mary shall accompany my trunks to Rothrage Castle and make sure my rooms are prepared for my arrival tomorrow. Everything is proceeding exactly as we planned."

Pouring a cup of tea, she noticed her brother's countenance had not improved. "Fitzwilliam, what is it? Are you cross with me?"

"Never," he said quickly. "It is nothing for you to be concerned over."

"Then there is something. Pray tell me or I shall worry. Is someone ill?" When he didn't answer, she continued, "Dear God, has another rumour been spread?" Her face was full of fear and she set her teacup down with trembling fingers.

"No, no, it is nothing like that. I am just a little distressed to be handing your care over to His Grace. I have been so used to being responsible for you that I fear I am not ready for you to leave me."

"Brother, how silly you are," Georgiana giggled, relieved it wasn't anything serious. "I would have thought you would be happy to be rid of such responsibility."

"Not if it means you will be so very far away from me."

"His Grace has promised we may visit whenever I

desire. In addition, we plan to spend a few weeks with you this fall. Besides, you have little Jane to care for now, have you not? She will be ready for her coming out in a mere fifteen years or so."

Fitzwilliam slumped in his chair and rubbed his temples. "Dearest, this is not helping."

Laughing, Georgiana went to her brother's side and unceremoniously wrapped her arms around him. "Fitzwilliam, you are the best of brothers. Please be happy for me. I could not be happier for myself. I have found my true love, just as you did."

"I am happy for you dearest; I am only a little sad for myself. I think I will miss you greatly."

"I shall miss you too, but I have no doubt that we will see each other very often."

"I hope so. Now, off with you. Eat your breakfast and let your brother sulk in peace."

At a quarter past ten, the Duke of Rothford arrived at the Darcy townhouse with two carriages. Georgiana's trunks were already brought down and waiting to be loaded when he knocked on the door and was let in. He did not have much time since he was expected early in Abingdon, but he wanted to make sure he had a few minutes with his future bride.

For a long minute, he stood looking intently into Georgiana's eyes. Then he brushed her lips with the lightest kiss and whispered, "Tomorrow you come *home*. The place where you belong. With me, forever."

The sixty miles from London to Rothrage Castle was little more than half a day's journey. They first stopped to rest the horses in Slough. The number of carriages on the road diminished the farther they removed from London, and by their second stop at Maidenhead they were making very good time. When they reached Henley on the Thame they ate a nice meal at the inn and changed horses. Georgiana was certain they would make it to Rothrage Castle before five o'clock at the pace they were going.

One mile outside of Wallingford their carriage slowed to a stop. They heard the driver speaking to someone. Fitzwilliam leaned out of the window to see who detained them. "It is His Grace," he reported to the ladies.

"It is very good to see you," the Duke said, bringing his horse close to the window.

"It is good to see you too," Georgiana said. "We are close to Rothrage Castle now, are we not?"

"Yes, you are just entering my property. It is another two miles to the castle." The Duke tipped his hat and gave her a radiant smile. "Follow my man." He waved the driver forward and the carriage began to move again. He kept pace atop his white gelding alongside the carriage. Through the open window, he and Georgiana shared frequent looks that spoke more than words could.

The carriage drew to a stop and the Duke dismounted to open the carriage door. You can see the castle from here. Come, I would like to show you."

Devin led Georgiana to a spot behind the carriage. Leaning close to her he said, "Welcome to our home."

Georgiana gazed in wonder at the picturesque scene before her. Even under an overcast sky, the noble edifice in the distance looked warm and inviting, nestled in a landscape as pretty as any she had ever known. "Never have I seen a place I could love as much as my beloved Pemberley until now. I am sure to be very happy here with you."

Devin turned her around in his arms and tilted her beautiful face towards his. "I love you, Georgiana Darcy."

"I love you, Devin." With a deep feeling of contentment, she accepted his kiss.

Chapter Twenty-Two

Georgiana could not decide if the morning of her wedding was pleasure, torture, or equal measures of both as she stood at her bedroom window and gazed into the rising sun. Though all of England was growing weary of the perpetual haze that had obscured the heavens since spring, she thought it made sunsets and sunrises truly spectacular. Her eyes were riveted to the symphony of pinks and oranges on the horizon. Surely such a beautiful beginning to the day was a good omen.

Mary helped her bathe and then dried her hair in front of an ornate fireplace she had never seen the likes of. No expense had been spared to maintain Rothrage Castle in the highest quality and comforts known to man, yet the family had refined tastes and nothing was ostentatious or gaudy. Georgiana thought the style perfectly matched what she knew of the Duke.

Once her hair was dry, her wedding clothes were laid out and Elizabeth came to help her dress. The cream gown fashioned from raw silk was more exquisite than any dress Georgiana had ever seen. The bodice and sleeves had an elegant border of off-white and gold beads sewn onto the fabric. Cream silk hung from the bodice to the floor. Beadwork began at her waist and increased in density until the fabric could scarcely be seen beneath the intricate design along the hem.

The dress was so ornate it could hardly be enhanced by jewellery, but a small string of pearls circled her ivory throat.

When Fitzwilliam came to escort her to the chapel, Georgiana stood in the middle of the room looking more grown up and beautiful than he had ever seen her. He could not help the fatherly tears that sprang to his eyes. Though he was not her father, he had raised her for most of her life and he took pride in the beautiful woman she had become.

"Georgie, dearest, you look bewitching," he said in a voice full of emotion. "I just sent a very excited and nervous bridegroom ahead to the chapel. We shall leave when you are ready. Would you like me to wait for you downstairs?"

"No, I am ready now. Moreover, I think I would get lost if you were not here to direct me down. I scarcely know how I came to the room last night."

"Do not fret; we shan't be lost along the way." Offering her his arm he said, "Shall we?"

Fitzwilliam led Georgiana through the castle with Elizabeth right behind them. Each step they took was heavier than the one before. As they reached the grand entrance, Georgiana caught her brother wiping a tear from his cheek. She was too overcome herself to remark upon it. She clung to her brother, not once letting go of his arm during the carriage ride from the castle to the church.

The chapel was larger than the one at Pemberley and much older. The double doors were slightly open and she could see the Duke's back as he stood at the front with the parson. He was striking in his black coat and breeches.

Elizabeth straightened Georgiana's skirts and handed her a bouquet. Her hands clenched nervously around the flower stems. She was excited. Incredibly so. Her heart raced when Elizabeth said she would go take her seat at the front, leaving her alone with her brother.

"This is it. Are you ready?" Fitzwilliam asked in a heavy voice.

"Yes, I am ready." Wiping a tear off her cheek, she said, "Fitzwilliam, I would not have survived without you. You are my rock, sturdy against every storm. You have saved me so many times."

He kissed her cheek and settled her hand in the crook of his elbow. Her gentle touch on his arm was a balm to his soul, and he wrapped his hand over hers to offer mutual support as the doors swung open and he walked her towards her future.

At the sound of the doors opening, everyone stood and the Duke of Rothford turned around. The closer they walked to the front the drier Georgiana's throat became. It was almost time.

A sigh escaped Fitzwilliam as he removed Georgiana's arm from his and gave her to the Duke. The air between them was thick with happiness and love. Georgiana hardly heard a word of the ceremony and had no idea whether she had responded properly. She must have made it through because she recognised when the parson pronounced them man and wife and asked them to sign the registry.

Georgiana returned up the aisle not on her brother's arm, but on her husband's. The pathway from the chapel to the carriages was lined with well-wishers and congratulations were offered from every person they passed.

The Duke helped his bride into the carriage and stepped up behind her before closing the door. Sitting next to him in the carriage, Georgiana looked deep into his eyes and saw all the love she could hope for and more.

Almost The End

Continue reading the final chapter in Ayr Bray's *Threat of Scandal* **for a glimpse of the newlyweds** *After the Wedding.*

The following chapter is for mature readers due to the explicit nature of the content.

Chapter Twenty-Three

The moment the carriage drove away from the church, the Duke of Rothford, now her Devin, brought his lips to hers in their first *real* kiss as man and wife. She had not even regained her breath and now he was taking it again. She was just beginning to return his kiss when he pressed his tongue to the seam of her lips and, at her grant of access, delved inside her mouth. She could taste him and smell his scent that she had already come to love. Georgiana tangled her hands in his thick hair and pressed her body against him. The contact of their bodies stoked the fire within her and she boldly slipped her tongue into his mouth as he had done to her.

Devin kissed her in the carriage as they rode back to the castle. He kissed her when the carriage stopped at the top of the drive with a clear view of their home. He kissed her as he eased her out of the carriage. It was a heady kiss neither of them wanted to end, but they knew a procession of carriages with guests for share it with a friend.

Recommend it. Please help others find this book by recommending it to friends, readers' groups, and discussion boards.

Review it. Please tell other readers you liked this book by reviewing it.

Thank you for your support!

Love,

Ayr

Ayr Bray's Novels

The Illegitimate Heir: The younger son of an earl often cannot afford to marry for love, so it is fortunate Colonel Richard Fitzwilliam has fallen in love with Helen Malham, who has both beauty and wealth. Her father, however, will not allow her to marry a man without a title.

When the Prince Regent names Richard the Duke of Blachedone, it is both a blessing and a curse. His newly acquired title means he may marry Helen—assuming she will have him once the truth comes out. He was awarded the dukedom not for his service to the Crown, but because he is the former duke's illegitimate son, and soon all of London will know.

Mr. Calvin Aldrich is a rake and a blackguard and set to be one of the richest dukes in England … until his uncle is stripped of his titles and possessions while on his deathbed. Bereft of his inheritance, Calvin will stop at nothing to get revenge on his uncle's illegitimate heir. He will strike at Richard in any way he can, even if it means ruining an innocent woman.

Available on Audiobook

Threat of Scandal: At twenty years of age, Georgiana Darcy embarks on her third season in London hoping to find true love. Things go terribly wrong when she is implicated in a scandalous affair with the Duke of Rothford and, though she is innocent of wrongdoing, London society shuns her and her reputation is in tatters.

For months the Duke has had troubles of his own; the last thing he needs is to be caught up in London's latest scandal with a perfect stranger. The Duke is an honourable man, however, and does his best to clear their names and restore Georgiana's reputation.

The Duke's kindness and attentiveness ignite the kind of love in Georgiana she's always dreamed of. She knows a peer of the realm could never marry a mere gentleman's daughter, so she contents herself with simply being near him. But when a new scandal arises, she must leave London and the Duke or risk losing her reputation forever.

Available on Audiobook

Pemberley Mistletoe: Fitzwilliam and Elizabeth Darcy had enjoyed a fortnight of being totally irresponsible with regards to anything other than matters of the heart, but the honeymoon is over, and Christmas is sneaking up on them. With the assistant of Mrs. Reynolds, Elizabeth decorates the manor and plans for an intimate holiday party of six, but little does she know how upside down those plans will turn when the party ends up with an additional thirteen uninvited guests.

Will Elizabeth Darcy be able to blend the Darcy and Bennet traditions into a holiday that both she and Fitzwilliam can enjoy, and can she do it while so many women are in attendance waiting for her to mess up.

HUNTED; I SURVIVED: Melanie Wells has a plan. As soon as graduation is over she will move into the perfect apartment, start the perfect job, and launch her perfect career. Everything is falling into place … until one wrong turn shatters her dreams.

After witnessing a drug smuggling operation, Melanie is tortured, shot, and left for dead. Her survival is nothing short of miraculous, but it may not last when the drug cartel finds out she's still alive and planning to testify against them.

Enter Thane Reeves, sexy as hell Private Security Consultant and former Army Ranger. For years he's loved Melanie from afar, and now he would risk anything, including his own life, to keep her safe.

Melanie's plan never included love. If anyone can change her mind it's Thane. He ignites a passion in her she didn't know she was capable of, but when you're running for your life it's easy to fall for your protector. Melanie can't be sure if her feelings for Thane are real, and with drug lords and contract killers gunning for her, she may not live long enough to find out.

Ayr Bray's Novellas

COWARDLY WITNESS; PEMBERLEY BOOK 1: Matthew Poe is the only witness in a case of murder and corruption in the lead mining industry. After an attempt is made on his life, he seeks refuge at Pemberley.

Mr. Darcy, bound by honour and duty to his King and country, agrees to take him in, though his presence puts everyone at Pemberley in danger—including Darcy's new bride, Elizabeth.

When Mr. Poe's secret is revealed with disastrous consequences, will Darcy succeed in protecting his loved ones and the witness, or will he be forced to choose between family and honour?

In *Cowardly Witness*, Ayr Bray masterfully creates a world around Pemberley electrified with the excitement and intrigue of a riveting suspense story.

SCENT of DESIRE: After a tempestuous acquaintance fraught with misconceptions, Elizabeth Bennet and Fitzwilliam Darcy are at last of one mind and heart. Their betrothal is not without its own difficulties, however, and a single misunderstanding may place all of their future happiness in jeopardy.

By Amazon Best-Selling author Ayr Bray, *Scent of Desire* is a *Pride and Prejudice* expansion chronicling the six-week engagement of one of the world's most beloved Jane Austen couples.

Available on Audiobook

Felicity in Marriage: Turn down the lights and indulge in the passionate scenes of Fitzwilliam and Elizabeth Darcy's first day married.

This book is not just hot and steamy, but sweet and romantic."

Moments after the parson pronounces Fitzwilliam and Elizabeth Darcy man and wife they kiss. That kiss may have been a chaste kiss in front of the parson, their families, and God, but what takes place the rest of the day, well that's between just the two of them.

Felicity in Marriage; An Erotic Pride and Prejudice Continuation (1) takes readers on an erotic and passion filled twenty-four hours with our newlyweds. Starting in the carriage on their ride back to Netherfield Park for the wedding brunch, and not ending until they make love in the master suite at London House.

Conjugal Obligation: *Conjugal Obligation; An Erotic Pride and Prejudice Continuation (2)* picks up where *Felicity in Marriage* left off. This book can be read independently or enjoyed as a sequel to *Felicity in Marriage*.

Twenty-four hours have passed since our newlyweds married and experienced their first night of conjugal felicity. Now it is time that they leave London for Pemberley.

Conjugal Obligation takes readers on an erotic and passion filled three days as our newlyweds travel from the Darcy's London residence to Pemberley. The trip is not all romantic interludes though when twenty miles into their journey they are waylaid when they come across a disabled carriage and a woman being brutally taken advantage of.

Mr. Darcy must display courage and strength to save, not only the woman, but Elizabeth as the ruffians pull her from the carriage.

In *Conjugal Obligation* Ayr Bray promises her readers not only the intense passion and love between her characters, but also introduces another of literature's couples that have a relationship that is a stark opposite. Ayr shows us a marriage of mind, body, and soul and then another where sexual relations are nothing more than a wife submitting to the carnal lusts and desires of her cruel husband.

Conjugal Obligation will take your breath away.

Magnetic: Before Samantha Lyle met Darren Riggs, she was a freshman at the University of Washington. She had just left her daddy's farm in Ritzville, and was ready to embrace the elegance and sophistication of big city life.

Her first day on campus was fraught with one catastrophe after another, but it gained her the attention of Darren, her gorgeous Greek God.

Darren's a junior on campus, and the two are magnetically drawn to one another. He stirs a passion in her that she's never felt before. She excites him as no woman ever has.

After saving her repeatedly, he requests dinner with her as payment for his chivalrous acts. Samantha accepts, but their seemingly perfect date turns sour when a woman from Darren's past shows up and confronts Samantha in the women's bathroom.

Will Samantha be able to look past the woman's accusations, or will she lose the man whom she was born to love?

Ayr Bray's Novelettes

Not Handsome Enough: Have you ever wondered what Mr. Darcy was thinking when he stood stoic and aloof during *Pride and Prejudice*?

In *Not Handsome Enough* Ayr Bray has answered your musings.

Moments after Fitzwilliam Darcy slights Elizabeth Bennet at the Meryton Assembly she commences telling the story to all in attendance. Forced to retreat to the quiet and solitude of the streets outside, he admits to himself that she was the unfortunate woman who his comments were directed at, however, any woman who had been sitting there would have received the same treatment. In reality, it was not her he was avoiding dancing with, but dancing in general.

A week passes and while sitting in Richard's Bookshop in Meryton he observes Miss Elizabeth Bennet and experiences his first daydream about her. That evening, while attending a party at the Lucas Lodge, he is desperate to remember his dream, but no matter how hard he tries, he cannot recall the details. Desperate to experience it again and swept away by her fine eyes and pretty face, he releases control and experiences the most sensual and erotic dream.

At its conclusion Mr. Darcy will do almost anything to speak to the love of his life.

Six Inches Deep in Mud: In Jane Austen's Pride and Prejudice the reader is left to wonder what Mr. Darcy was thinking when he stood stoic and aloof.

In *Six Inches Deep in Mud* Ayr Bray has answered your musings.

Six Inches Deep in Mud begins as Mr. Darcy attends Mr. Bingley on an outing to dine with the officers. An event that he had not anticipated being enjoyable, but that turns out well, despite his apprehensions.

While they are out, Miss Caroline Bingley invites Miss Jane Bennet to tea. When she shows up, on horseback, in the rain, she takes ill and must remain at Netherfield.

The following morning, Mr. Darcy is out with the Netherfield steward assessing the fence line's state of disrepair. He notices Miss Elizabeth Bennet making her way toward Netherfield. Watching her for a few moments, his mind is thrown into a dream that tempts the limits of his desires.

Will Mr. Darcy succumb to the temptations that his wife, Elizabeth Darcy lays before him, or will he withstand her charms?

Succession of Rain: Have you ever wondered what Mr. Darcy was doing during the four days of incessant rain leading up to the Netherfield ball?

In *Succession of Rain* Ayr Bray has answered your musings.

Succession of Rain begins the day Mr. Bingley and his sisters offer personal invitations to the local families for their ball at Netherfield. Mr. Darcy, still upset by his encounter with Mr. Wickham on the streets of Meryton, stays behind, allowing his disposition to become dark and foreboding.

For four days Darcy is left to the wanderings of his mind and his passion-filled dreams of Elizabeth Bennet.

By the night of the Netherfield ball, he has indulged in her womanly pleasures more than once in his dreams, and he is now determined to dance with her.

Will the night end with Elizabeth continuing to plague his dreams, or will he push her from his mind forever?

Made in the USA
Lexington, KY
07 May 2016